Perfectly in Tune

Jenny Worstall

For music teachers everywhere

Contents

Chapter 1

According to legend, the ring finger has a vein that connects directly to the heart.

I stared at my left hand, remembering the weight of the sparkling diamond I had been so proud to wear, and the promises Charles had made to me of a glittering future, full of love and hope.

The bright autumn landscape flashed past the window as I moved with the rhythm of the train wheels, clunketty clunk, clunketty clunk.

The Wiltshire countryside was so beautiful at this time of year, with its fields and meadows almost completely recovered. 1976 would be famous one day for its drought, and surely the hottest summer in living memory. Far in the distance, I spotted a threatening storm cloud scudding our way. We could have done with that in August when there was scarcely enough water for a three inch bath.

The waiter pushed his trolley down the corridor outside, then opened the smeary glass door of my compartment.

"Refreshments? Tea? Coffee?"

"Tea please, with milk but no sugar."

I accepted the cup gratefully, putting my hands around its comforting warmth.

"Soon be at Salisbury. We usually get many more passengers there – won't have the carriage to yourself after that. You have a good day, Miss."

Tears sprang to my eyes; it didn't take much to set me off these days. A kind word from a stranger, a cheerful glance – the sight of my bare hand where once there had been an enormous engagement ring.

It had been two years since Charles and I had become engaged and one year since he had broken it off.

"It's not you, it's me," he'd explained on the phone. "Doesn't feel right anymore; besides, I've met someone else. Funny thing is, you introduced us. She's one of your best friends – from your village."

Charles had married his 'someone else' five months ago, in the pretty country church in my parents' parish – a double betrayal, Charles and my friend, which I was still struggling to come to terms with.

"So pleased to get on before the downpour..." a voice said.

"Room for another?"

"Do you mind if I sit here?"

I hadn't even noticed the train had stopped at Salisbury.

"Be my guest! Plenty of space." I scooted along

towards the window. "I'll just budge up..."

I hastily swung my grip into the overhead rack and cradled my handbag. Very soon the whole carriage was full and two long rows of strangers faced each other, shoulders tightly squeezed together. The springs of the tartan upholstery groaned under the extra weight.

Then the door was pulled sideways again and a diminutive nun peered in. She looked quite tired, poor thing, and I wondered whether she was bound for St Cecilia's like me. Perhaps we'd be able to share a taxi from Gillingham if that were the case.

My contact lenses were still swimming around my eyes in an alarming fashion, making my vision a little blurry – tended to happen after a tearful episode – and I squinted at her habit. She had a sort of cape thing over the top, with large metal buttons. Mm, didn't look quite the same as the uniform the nuns at St Cecilia's Convent School wore, so probably not on her way there to join the community. Unless she was a visitor? I stifled a giggle. My nosiness was getting completely out of control.

The nun took a deep breath and began to close the door again; there wasn't a square inch of the bench left for her.

"Please, take my seat, Sister," a gallant gentleman sitting next to the door said. "I have such happy memories of being taught by nuns when I was evacuated as a small boy in the War. No, really – I insist!"

"Thank you; you are most kind," the nun said and the gentleman eased past her to the corridor and unfolded his newspaper, allowing her to slip into his seat.

I could hear snippets of conversation as the nun chattered away to her neighbour, a frazzled looking lady with a couple of lively children.

"Yes, I've come a long way – from Rome, as it happens," the nun said. "Flew in earlier, then travelled across London and caught the train from Waterloo."

"Goodness! You must be tired! Stop that, you two – oh, sorry Sister – my kids will be the death of me. They get that bored when we travel back from a Sunday afternoon visit to my mum..."

"No bother, I assure you...and I'm Sister Claire...so nice to meet you and your charming children."

"That looks an interesting book, Sister Claire. Very long!"

"Yes, fascinating, all about travelling in America – not that I've ever been there. Oh look, is that Tisbury we're coming into? My stop's the next one after this."

After a while I fell into a light doze, waking with a start when we reached Gillingham. Most of the passengers had already got off – there was just the lady with her two children left in the carriage.

"My stop!" I screeched.

"Here, let me help you," the lady said, wrestling the door of the compartment open for me.

"Thanks!" I said, grabbing my bags and hurtling through the carriage door and onto the platform in the nick of time.

I looked up and down to see if I could see the nun. She must have got off while I was still asleep. Perhaps she'd already left the station?

I still wondered if she was on her way to St Cecilia's. The mention of her name, Sister Claire, rang a vague sort of bell in my mind, but I couldn't quite place it. Ah, wait a minute; yes, in our last Assembly before the break Reverend Mother had said something about a nun who was journeying from abroad to visit the school for the second half of term. I had been frantically searching through my music for the accompaniment to the next hymn at the time and hadn't been listening that closely. Had Reverend Mother revealed why the nun would be visiting?

Once outside I made a beeline for the taxi rank.

"St Cecilia's Convent, please," I said, leaning into the front window of the nearest cab. "No, it's fine thanks; I can manage to have my bags in the back, no worries."

As we sped along the country lanes, the driver gave me a curious look in the mirror.

"Got it!" he said triumphantly. "I know who you are. You're that music teacher from the convent – you conducted the outstanding concert my wife and I went to in the School Hall last summer. My daughter was in the choir."

"Yes, that's me! Guilty as charged. So pleased

you enjoyed the concert. Remind me, what's your daughter's name? Oh, yes, beautiful voice, and such a lovely girl...and do you and your wife sing? I'm always looking for extra voices for the choir. So many of the parents live miles away or even abroad, so we do tend to rely on the parents of the day girls."

"I'm a bass, as it happens, and the wife's an alto; we love a good sing."

"Splendid! I'll jot down a few details for you – I've got a notebook somewhere in my bag...choir rehearsals are on Tuesday evenings. I hope you can make it."

The taxi driver prattled on for ages about what a wonderful school St Cecilia's was and how happy he and his family were that his daughter had managed to obtain a place there as a day girl.

"One thing, though," he said. "The day girls – they don't always get treated quite right by the boarders."

I sat forward. I'd heard about this sort of thing before and was determined to do something to stamp it out. Injustice of any kind was something I found hard to tolerate. "Tell me more. What's been going on?"

"Well." He cleared his throat. "The boarders call the day girls 'Day Bugs' and throw things at them in class when the teacher's not looking – which seems to be quite a lot of the time."

I could imagine that. Some of the teaching nuns were fairly elderly with decidedly dodgy eyesight and hearing. It was a wonder some of them were still working, but nuns never quite retire.

"There was an incident last week, out on the hockey pitch, where a gang of boarders rounded on my girl and pushed her about, accusing her of thinking she was something special because she got to go home at night, unlike them."

"Leave it with me," I said grimly. "I'll make sure Reverend Mother gets to hear about this."

"I wouldn't mind," the driver said, "but if they could see where we live, our little cottage, they'd know there's nothing to be jealous of. I've heard some of the girls live in mansions when they're home with their parents. It's rumoured one of the girls even has a moat around her house."

"But it's not where you live that's important, is it?" I said. "These boarders might be jealous because the day girls return to a loving home at night with their own things all around them. They have the freedom to potter about and have a snack whenever they want and snuggle up to their parents for a cuddle."

"When you put it like that, I suppose it makes more sense," the driver said. "Tell you what, don't say anything to Reverend Mother. I'm feeling sorry for the boarders now – don't want them to get into trouble. I'll have a word with my daughter about being understanding."

"And sticking up for herself?"

The taxi man grinned at me in the mirror. "That too! Definitely."

The journey continued through glorious countryside until we swung through the gates of the School.

"I say – you didn't happen to see a nun coming out of the station, did you?" I asked.

"Yes, she came out shortly before you did," the driver replied.

"Was she waiting for a taxi too?"

"Well now you mention it, I thought she was at first – she started walking towards me – then she started talking to another lady and went off round the side with her, I presumed to the car park."

St Cecilia's was before us now in its full glory, the myriad tiny windows winking in the autumn sunshine.

"Doesn't it look a picture?" the taxi man said. "Did you know it was a famous country house hotel back in the thirties? Right up to the start of the War."

"I've heard that from the nuns," I replied. "Wouldn't it have been great to have been a guest here?"

"Yes – and just imagine all the taxi cabs in those days whizzing up and down the drive with society folk coming for a stay in the country."

"Wow! I can picture it now."

"If buildings could talk, we'd hear some tales all right! Now Miss Gold, are you sure you can manage your luggage?"

"I'm fine, thank you. Enjoy the rest of your weekend – goodbye!"

I walked towards the front door. Staying with my parents in Surrey for half term had been smashing, but now it was back to work. The second half of the autumn term was always the busiest part of the whole year for music teachers. Goodness, there was even going to be someone turning up to be interviewed for the post of violin teacher this very afternoon. No rest for the wicked! I pulled my shoulders back and rang the bell.

"Hello, my dear Flora!" Reverend Mother's cheerful face appeared before me and she drew me into a warm embrace. "I've put a hot water bottle in your bed to air it and staff supper will be served in an hour or so. Did you have a good break? You must tell me all about it. How were your parents? Did you go to any concerts in London? Meet anyone special? Come into the warmth my dear – I've a surprise for you."

I followed Reverend Mother into the panelled Entrance Hall, inhaling the familiar beeswax fragrance emanating from all the wooden surfaces. I couldn't wait to get up to the safety of my cosy little room in the staff quarters on the top floor and unpack my things, but I'd better see what Reverend Mother's mysterious surprise was first. I looked down for a moment. I was rather wary of unexpected events after the shock of my broken engagement, preferring life to be steady and even dull – to feel safe. Would I ever recover from the bombshell of Charles' betrayal?

A sudden raft of sunlight burst through the

stained glass window over the wide staircase and in the distance I noticed a tall stranger standing by the fireplace, his fair hair glowing and his piercing cornflower blue eyes shining.

I took a deep breath. Maybe, given time, I would be able to embrace life again. Very softly, my heart began to hum fragments of a tune I had thought I would never hear again.

Chapter 2

"Hello, I'm Joe Oak," the vision said, holding out a hand. "Frightfully sorry to be so early for the interview."

I stood rooted to the spot.

"Mr Oak's applied for the violin teaching post," Reverend Mother explained.

"I, I gathered that," I mumbled and then, recovering my manners, held out my hand. "How do you do?"

How could he be a violin teacher? He looked like a film star!

Joe Oak's hand felt warm and friendly – and dangerous. I determined to keep my wits about me; I would not be taken in by a man again in a hurry.

"Perhaps you'd like to put your bags upstairs, Flora dear," Reverend Mother said, "while I show Mr Oak to the Blue Parlour. Come down when you're ready and I'll have tea waiting."

Nodding, I raced up the stairs to Slum Alley, which was what we called the staff quarters in the attics, and dumped my bags in my room.

"Hi!" came a voice from the kitchenette next door. "Had a good half term?"

"What on earth are you doing here, Susie?" I said. "You should be at home with your daughter on a Sunday."

Susie bustled into the corridor holding a mop. "The nuns needed some extra help getting everything ready for the second half of term; I've been busy in the dormitories all afternoon."

"On a Sunday? Way beyond the call of duty," I said.

"Suppose so." Susie sighed. "But it keeps me busy. Anyway, I've nearly finished up here, then that's me done. I'll be off home to my Diana, to see if she's finished her half term homework. No idea why she always leaves it to the night before term starts again. Then I'll cook a nice supper for the two of us and we'll have an evening in front of the telly."

"Don't you let Reverend Mother take advantage of you," I said.

Susie shook her head. "You don't know how good she's been to me. There was a time when I wondered what was to become of me, I really did, and Reverend Mother, well, let's just say she helped me out in my hour of need. I'll let you get on now – you look as if you're in a hurry."

"It isn't that I don't want to chat," I said, "but the candidate for the violin job has turned up early. Reverend Mother's making tea and I'm supposed to be on my way down." I fiddled with the cuff of my blouse. "Oh, Susie – he's so good looking! I was expecting someone much older and ordinary looking, but this guy, well, he's drop dead gorgeous."

Susie threw her head back and roared with laughter. "Well, Flora, what are you waiting for? Better get down there straight away."

"Not before I've put some lipstick on," I said, rushing back to my room. "I'll catch up with you tomorrow and tell you how it went, promise."

"I'll hold you to that," Susie called after me.

Downstairs in the Blue Parlour, Reverend Mother had a beautiful tea organised on a silver tray.

"Milk?" she asked Joe.

"Yes please. And no sugar. Thank you."

The thin china cup looked so tiny and fragile as he wrapped his long fingers around it. I felt sure he would be able to crush it with very little effort if he put his mind to it.

"You have a glowing reference from your last school," Reverend Mother said. "What makes you want to leave and move down here?"

"I really enjoyed teaching up in Yorkshire," Joe explained. "The school was fantastic and the boys were great – so inquisitive and lively. I felt I learnt just as much from them as they did from me."

Reverend Mother nodded.

"But I wanted to move back to Dorset. It's where I grew up and my family still live here – my parents have a house in town and I'm staying with them at the moment, hoping to get my own place in time. I left the school in Harrogate at the end of the summer term and I've been doing some private teaching locally and freelance work, but now I think I'm ready for the challenge of teaching in a school again. When I saw this job advertised, I was immediately interested."

Reverend Mother put her tea cup and saucer down on the table and turned to me.

"You mentioned the boys at your previous school," I said. "Have you any experience of teaching girls?"

"No," Joe said. "They can't be that different, surely?"

Reverend Mother raised an eyebrow. "They can be challenging, in their own way – particularly for the male staff. At least, that's what we find here."

Especially challenging if the male in question happens to look like a Greek god.

"Have a macaroon." Reverend Mother offered a delicate china plate of crumbly biscuits to Joe.

"Thank you!"

"Made in our own kitchen," she said. "You would of course be welcome to have your meals here while you are working."

Just then a small group of girls in tartan skirts ran past the window, squealing merrily.

"Ah, a few early returners," Reverend Mother said. "They should know they're not allowed on the Nun's Lawn, though. Excuse me, while I go and have a word."

An awkward silence descended, then Joe and I started talking at once.

"How long have you been..." he asked

"Are you enjoying being back..?" I said.

We both laughed and he indicated that I should speak first.

"I was wondering if you're enjoying being back near your family."

"Oh yes! Harrogate was great, but I've always wanted to move back here," Joe said. "My sister and her family live near my parents and it's been good to feel part of the family again. Just like old times. I had a great half term entertaining my sister's children."

"You know we're looking for someone to start straight away, don't you?" I asked.

"Yes," Joe said. "I was going to ask about that. I mean, I'm happy to start whenever and I can fit in the two days you're offering with my other work, no problem, but I did wonder why the job was suddenly vacant."

Time to be truthful.

"The previous teacher couldn't cope," I said. "The girls ran rings round him."

Joe leaned forward. "What sort of things did they do?"

"One girl used to take the top string off her violin before every lesson and pretend she didn't know what had happened to it. Another used to feign deafness so that the teacher ended up shouting himself hoarse. The final straw was when all the girls turned up to orchestra wearing their pyjamas. The poor man was so overwrought he gave his notice in immediately, the week before half term, which has left us in a bit of a pickle."

Joe chortled. "Are you interviewing many other musicians?"

"Not exactly," I said, "because you're the only person that's applied. Most people aren't free to start at such short notice I suppose."

Or they have heard what the girls at St Cecilia's are like.

A sudden commotion caused us both to look out of the French windows.

In the middle of the Nun's Lawn, Reverend Mother was pointing a stern finger at the trespassers who stood with their heads bowed. As soon as she turned back to the building, we could see the girls speeding away, hair flying, no doubt in search of fresh mischief.

Joe grinned. "Seem a lively bunch!"

"You don't know the half of it!"

Reverend Mother glided back into the room.

"Now, would you like to stay for staff supper, Mr Oak?"

"Why yes, that would be lovely; many thanks."

"Good. Then later I will have a chat with Miss Gold and we hope to have good news for you after that. If we were to offer you the job, would you accept?"

"Well, yes," Joe said. "I would be delighted to."

"Flora, perhaps you would like to show Mr Oak around the Music Department?" Reverend Mother suggested.

"Of course," I said. "It would be a pleasure. This

way, please."

As we walked through the Hall on our way to the Music Department – a grand title for what was in reality a rather small hut behind the Hall – I said, "Please do call me Flora. Miss Gold sounds so formal."

"Flora it is, then," he said.

I thought my name had never sounded as sweet.

"And please call me Joe," he added.

As we went out of the door at the back of Hall, we had to descend a steep staircase and go through the Undercroft. It was quite dark down there and I accidentally tripped and bumped into Joe as we walked across the uneven tiled floor.

"Steady!" he said, holding out his arm. "You OK?"

"Fine!" I squeaked.

Why did my voice sound so puny? Why was my heart beating so furiously? I already knew the answer to that.

I was soon showing him round the glories of the Music Hut.

"Cosy!" Joe said. "Nothing like the school in Harrogate where I taught."

There were rows of embroidered cushions scattered on the benches, a box record player, a neat shelf of music history books and a highly polished upright piano in the corner.

"What was your last school like?" I asked.

"Oh, everything all over the place," Joe said. "You were quite likely to find a muddy football boot on a chair or an ink splodge on the floor. I can already see St Cecilia's is impressively well ordered."

I laughed. "I noticed that when I first arrived, but now I take it for granted. The nuns are very keen on tidiness. And shininess. They polish everything they can – to within an inch of its life."

Joe and I locked eyes for a moment. I could see our reflection in the glass of the window at the side; he was so tall my head only came up to his shoulder. I dug my nails into my palm. Time to get a grip. It was no good falling for someone who'd let you down. Again.

"I could show you where the violin lessons take place," I offered. "Where you'd be teaching, if you get the job – if you still want it!"

I opened a door at the side of the main teaching room to reveal a much smaller room, little more than a glorified cupboard. It contained an upright piano, a chair and a music stand.

"It's got a lovely view in the daytime," I said. "You can see right down into the woods. The colours are glorious at this time of year."

"What's that?" Joe asked.

I put my head on one side.

"I can't hear anything – oh wait, I think I know what you're talking about."

There was a rustling sound from outside.

"That's the wind," I said. "You get used to it when you live up here."

Then we heard a roaring sound.

I chuckled. "That's a car. I'm sure you've heard

one of those before! Coming up the drive. More of the girls returning. Soon it'll be non-stop up and down the drive until everyone's back and ready to start the rest of the term. I can take you to the Dining Room for Staff Supper now – if you feel brave enough."

"Bring it on," Joe said. "I'm not frightened of anything!"

He might not have been frightened of anything but I was feeling increasingly alarmed. I already felt a strong attraction to him, yet I wasn't ready to trust again after Charles. If Joe started working at St Cecilia's, how would I cope?

Chapter 3

I led Joe back through the Undercroft, taking care not to stumble into him again as we ascended the narrow staircase to the Hall.

"Who is your favourite composer, Mr Oak?" I asked.

I could do it – I could keep a professional distance.

"Er, not sure I have one," he said. "Do you? I mean, there are so many, all wonderful...and hadn't we agreed you were going to call me Joe?"

I walked a little faster, slipping in a patch of polish the nuns had forgotten to massage into the ancient floorboards, but managing to steady my balance before I skied across the Hall. That would have been an awkward look.

"Of course," I said. "Joe it is. And, er, no, in fact I don't actually have a favourite composer either, although I am very fond of Bach. And I love jazz."

Joe smiled and put his thumb up.

"Maybe you'd like to try the piano," I offered, indicating the vintage Steinway in the corner.

"OK, but I'm not that much of a pianist – you might have to help me out."

Joe flopped onto the lower end of the duet stool and began to vamp a bass line that was so irresistible, my fingers felt compelled to fly to the top of the keyboard and improvise a joyful jaunty tune. At first I played standing up but I didn't want to pull a muscle in my back and so I sat down beside him. The melodies and rhythms flowed like honey. We continued to play for a few minutes, our shoulders rubbing, counting and breathing as one, before laughter forced us to stop.

So much for keeping my distance.

On our way to Staff Supper, through the shadowy Entrance Hall, I saw Reverend Mother standing next to another nun who was dressed in an outdoor cape, a wimple covering her hair and ears.

"Flora! Mr Oak! Allow me to introduce you to Sister Claire. She's come to stay at the convent for a while, for a sabbatical. All the way from Rome."

Sister Claire! I'd forgotten about her. I screwed up my eyes; having short sight was incredibly annoying when you were as nosy as I was. Ah yes. Sister Claire – I recognised her from the strange cape she had been wearing on the train. The buttons on the front were very distinctive, large and shiny, made of some sort of silvery metal. And there was a large gap where one of them was missing.

"Nice to see you again, Sister Claire," I said.

"You've met before?" Reverend Mother put her head on one side, while Sister Claire remained completely still.

"Not met, as such, but I saw Sister Claire on the train," I explained.

Sister Claire gave a slight incline of her head and smirked.

"I looked for you when you came out of the station," I said. "It did cross my mind to ask whether you were travelling to St Cecilia's and I thought you might have wanted to share a lift. The taxi driver told me he'd seen a nun coming out of the station but then he said something about seeing someone else...he thought you had been about to ask him for a lift before another lady talked to you..."

My voice trailed away. Why couldn't I stop gabbling? Sister Claire was looking a little uncomfortable now – she must think I was stalking her or something. Poor woman – she was a visitor and I was behaving as if I had the right to poke my nose into her every move.

"Sorry to go on..." I murmured.

Sister Claire bobbed her head and a faint smile appeared on her lips.

My shoulders relaxed. She didn't seem to mind my inquisitiveness, so that was all right. My mother had always said I was one of the nosiest people she had ever met, to the point that she couldn't believe I was her daughter sometimes. Apparently from a very early age I had touched everything I shouldn't, opening cupboards and drawers to find what was inside. My first word had been, 'Why?' and my second, 'How?'

Reverend Mother suggested I took Joe to the

Dining Room. "Mr Oak, you won't mind a simple supper I hope on a Sunday evening? You will find we live very plainly here, but the food is wholesome and nourishing."

"I'm sure it will be delicious," he said.

I crossed my fingers behind my back.

As I showed Joe into the Dining Room, I whispered, "Sometimes it isn't all that delicious you know. Unless, that is, you like over-cooked cauliflower cheese and gristly rissoles..."

"Love them!" Joe winked at me.

Once we were seated at the battered mahogany table, and I had introduced Joe to the few other members of staff who were hungry enough to appear for supper, an ancient nun sidled into the room pushing a wobbly wooden trolley, the metal dishes with their misshapen lids clanking and clattering with the rhythm of the wonky wheels.

"Cauliflower cheese and rissoles," the nun announced as she lifted the lids of two of the casseroles with a flourish worthy of the top waiter in a five star Michelin restaurant.

Murmurs of, "Thank you, Sister," "How kind," and "What a delicious smell!" ran round the table before Joe announced, "My absolute favourite, Sister. How did you know?"

She cackled to hear this and waggled her finger, saying, "But that's not all!" She lifted the lid of the final dish to reveal a congealed mess with a thick orange crust around the edge. "Baked beans!"

Several staff members averted their eyes at this

point. The nun departed, her job done, and Joe and I took our places in the queue, plates in hand, to help ourselves to the delicacies.

"No Sunday evening at St Cecilia's is complete without baked beans," I said to Joe.

"Yes," another member of staff said. "We think they boil up all the left-over ones from the previous week especially for us as a treat."

"The fish and chip shop in the town does a roaring trade on Sunday evenings with plenty of custom from the staff here," another said.

"Please! Stop exaggerating!" I rolled my eyes in mock despair. "Don't put Joe off the place."

After all, I was rather hoping he would be coming to work here. With me. We could make sweet music...oh dear. There I went again, forgetting all my good intentions.

"Flora? Might I have a word?" Reverend Mother's head appeared round the door, her eyes widening in delight when they alighted on the rissoles. "So sorry everyone to disturb your supper time. I hope you are having a good meal?"

"Oh, yes."

"Thank you, Reverend Mother."

"It's delicious!"

"Love rissoles..."

I stepped outside with Reverend Mother. Would this be good news?

"I've been talking to the other nuns and we would like to offer Mr Oak the post of violin teacher – does that suit you, my dear? I don't want to appoint anyone you might feel won't quite cope."

"Yes! Oh, yes! He's amazing! I mean, I'm sure he'll fit in very well at St Cecilia's and his references were excellent; he was very happy with the teaching room I showed him too. He seems, well, perfect! I mean suitable..."

"Excellent!" Reverend Mother gave me a searching look – her speciality – and I dropped my eyes to the ground.

"Well then," she said, "why don't you tell him the good news, and when he's finished his meal, the three of us can have a quick chat and sort out a few details – which day he can start and so on. All right?"

More than all right! This was the best news I'd heard for ages.

As we stood there, Sister Claire emerged from a door a little further down the corridor, standing directly under a light and raising her hand in greeting.

She didn't look as neat and tidy as when I'd seen her on the train and seemed quite stressed, her face showing deep lines; her habit had ruffled up and I could see her ankles in their thick black tights as she turned and sped off round the corner.

"How long is Sister Claire staying?" I asked Reverend Mother.

"Until the end of term – and I know why you're asking."

"You do?"

Oh dear. The secret of my nosy nature was obviously not as hidden as I had imagined. I was mortified that Reverend Mother had noticed me scrutinising Sister Claire's appearance.

"Yes," she continued. "This is the time of year you're always on the lookout for extra singers for the choir, isn't it?"

This wasn't what had piqued my interest in Sister Claire – my curiosity was more to do with a total inability to mind my own business. However, it was true that I did a mean line in recruitment for the adult section of our school choir in the run up to Christmas. The press gang had nothing on me.

"Well, now you come to mention it," I said, "I do need more singers. Only this afternoon I was talking to the taxi driver about it on my way back from Gillingham – he seemed to think he and his wife would like to join the choir."

"Superb!" Reverend Mother said. "And of course, I will round up as many of the community as possible. They do enjoy singing in the Carol Concert. The Headmistress thought the concert last year was of West End standard."

An appreciative comment – but I wouldn't let it go to my head as I wasn't sure how familiar the nuns were with professional standards in the creative arts industry.

"Do you think Sister Claire might want to sing in the choir?" I asked.

Reverend Mother put her head on one side. "Well, she might need a little persuasion. I'm not sure she's a singer, as such. She certainly doesn't have a very loud voice – so far she's mostly whispered in any conversations we've had. Seems a little bashful and shy."

"Maybe she's getting a sore throat?" I suggested. "She was chatting away on the train to the lady next to her."

"That must be it," Reverend Mother said. "Worn her voice out."

It sounded a reasonable enough explanation. But there was another possibility. Did Sister Claire sound different because she was in reality someone else? What if she wasn't the same person as the nun on the train?

I dismissed the thought immediately. Preposterous! Ludicrous beyond belief. As my mother had often warned me, my vivid imagination was going to get me into a whole heap of trouble one of these fine days.

Chapter 4

"Pinch punch, first day of the month!"

"November! At last!"

"So glad to be back after half term!"

"Yippee! Not long until you-know-what!"

"Settle down girls," I said. "Yes, it's exciting that November's here and you're right, it won't be long until Christmas, but we need to get on with learning the descant for this carol."

I gulped. The second half of the autumn term always went in a flash and we had so much to get ready for the Carol Concert. A wave of tiredness swept over me – I'd been disturbed by a particularly vivid dream about Joe last night. It had started out as an enchanting romantic story, quickly becoming very complicated when unfortunately Joe morphed into Charles and I was dumped all over again. I'd woken miserable and despondent at three o'clock in the morning and hadn't been able to sleep properly after that.

"What page are we on?"

"Which carol are we singing?"

"Is it break time yet?"

"Quiet!" I roared. "Thank you. That's better.

Now, let's take it from the top."

I played the introduction and then half stood at the piano to conduct the girls in.

"Lovely! Come on seconds, you can sing louder than that...last verse now, so let's hear that descant."

The lesson ended at last and I escaped to the Staff Room for a restorative coffee. Susie was there handing round a plate of shortbread.

"Fresh from the oven," she said. "The Upper 3s really enjoyed making this. Shame they insisted on green icing, though. I've always been very fond of green, but it doesn't look right on shortbread."

As well as being the general skivvy, cleaning and polishing as needed, Susie often stood in for absent teachers; this morning she'd been taking a cookery lesson.

"I don't know how you cope, Susie," I said. "The girls were even livelier than usual today in my lesson. I feel wiped out – and I've only been back in the classroom for one morning."

We sat down side by side on the long shabby leather sofa.

"How did you get on with the violin teacher?" Susie asked. "You promised to tell me all about it."

"He's been offered the job and accepted."

"Quick work!" Susie said. "And when does he start?"

"Tomorrow. He won't be working here every day, because he has quite a few other musical commitments; in fact, it might get tricky at times because I think he'll be coming in on different days some weeks, but I'm sure I'll be able to work out a timetable."

Susie patted my arm. "You can do anything you set your mind to," she said. "You know how pleased Reverend Mother always is with your work."

"Thanks for the vote of confidence," I said. "I'm teaching your Diana after break; looking forward to a bit of peace and quiet after that singing lesson with the Upper 4s."

Susie's daughter Diana was in the sixth form at St Cecilia's and was my sole pupil for A level music this year. She was a delightful girl, easy going and sensible – very like her mother.

"I made sure she did all her homework," Susie said, "although she got a little stuck on the harmony you set her. Sadly, I can't help her with that at all, so she has to get on with it herself. It was a different matter when my Bob was alive – he was so musical and was able to help her with her piano practice and so on."

"I'm sure he'd be proud of how you and Diana have coped," I said gently.

Susie's husband Bob had died two years ago – sudden heart attack – and I had taken the school choir to sing at his funeral. Ever since then, Susie and I had been firm friends, despite the age difference.

"I'm relying on you to come to choir tomorrow," I said. "We need all the altos we can get! I've tried to get Sister Claire to come, but Reverend Mother seemed to think it wouldn't be her sort of thing."

"Oh yes, I've met Sister Claire," Susie said. "Very shy, isn't she? I said hello and introduced myself to her in the corridor on my way to teach this morning and she nearly jumped out of her skin. Wonder if she has some sort of nervous problem?"

"She's probably exhausted from her journey," I said. "It's a long way from Rome."

"That'll be it," Susie said. "Oh look – here she is. Why don't you ask her if she'd like to sing in the choir?"

Sister Claire was standing in the doorway of the Staff Room, peering about and wringing her hands.

"Good idea," I said. "I say! Sister Claire, would you like to sit here, with us?"

She sat down at the far end of the sofa and Susie rushed off to get her a coffee.

"What do you think about joining the choir," I asked.

"Not my thing," she said quietly.

"Oh, go on," Susie said, handing her a cup and saucer. "If I can manage to sing in it, you can."

"You sing in the choir?" Sister Claire pronounced the 'r' at the end of choir in an odd way, emphasising the consonant; must be a consequence of living abroad for so long.

"Yes, I do – in the altos," Susie said. "You're welcome to sit next to me, if that would make you feel more at home."

"I've changed my mind. I will join the choir – as long as I can sit next to you. Thank you."

Later, after lunch, I took a quick walk round the grounds in an attempt to get rid of a headache – the lack of sleep was catching up with me in a ferocious way. The weather was pretty cold and my hands were beginning to freeze. I reached into the pocket of my coat for my gloves – not there. What could I have done with them? I racked my brains. Did I leave them at my parents' house? No, I was sure I'd had them for the journey down yesterday. I definitely had them in the train, because I could remember them being on my lap when I was sitting in the carriage. Oh dear, I did get out of the train in a bit of a panic, nearly missing the station. Maybe I dropped them on the platform?

Reverend Mother was also out for a stroll. "All right, dear?" she asked as we met on the path by the woods. "You look a little peaky."

"Just a nasty headache brewing."

"The fresh air will do you good," she said. "Let's walk together."

We crunched along the gravel, our feet in time with each other.

"And I'm annoyed with myself too," I said, "because I think I left my gloves at the station yesterday."

"Why don't you call and see if they were handed in? One of the sixth formers is arriving back at school this evening by taxi – her flight from Athens was cancelled and she's a day late returning to school. The station master is very obliging and if he finds your gloves I'm sure he wouldn't mind giving them to the taxi driver."

"I'll do that," I said. "Thanks for the suggestion. I'll go and ring now."

It took me ages to get through to the station; I nearly gave up because I could see the clock ticking perilously close to my next lesson, but eventually the phone was answered.

"Hello," I said. "I'm ringing to enquire about my leather gloves..."

"Just a minute," the voice came. "Let me get the lost property box out...here we are. Now, there's a paperback book, but it doesn't look much good. Been in a puddle too by the look of it."

"No, not that," I said.

"A cheese sandwich – I think I'll throw that away as it's been here for a few days...a shoe lace, a knitting needle and that's it, I'm afraid. Oh, wait, there's one more thing – a large metal button. Someone handed this in today. Said they'd found it in the car park. Very odd looking thing. Now, what was it you've lost?"

"Gloves," I said. "But thank you so much for your help."

"My pleasure. Goodbye."

Ah well. It wasn't the end of the world. No doubt I could find some woollen mittens to replace them in town next weekend.

Afternoon lessons were relatively calm. I managed to get the Lower 4s to sit still and write the words for their Christmas carols – it would be much noisier the next time I saw them, when they would be working on the melodies and chords.

"Miss Gold? What rhymes with robin?"

"Do the words have to rhyme? I didn't know that."

"Do you have to have a chorus?"

"Is one verse too short?"

"The only rhyme I know for stable is table – do you think there would have been a table in Bethlehem? In the stable?"

"Does anyone have a pencil sharpener I can borrow?"

"Shh! Miss Gold's got her head on her desk. I think she's asleep."

I wasn't asleep, merely resting my eyes. I'd been thinking how my work at St Cecilia's had been a rock to cling onto after all the emotional upheaval of my broken engagement; the whole community here had been so supportive, showing me kindness and sympathy, without prying or judging. I was very lucky. And I owed Reverend Mother in particular a real debt of gratitude. It had been interesting hearing Susie say yesterday up in Slum Alley that Reverend Mother had helped her out in her hour of need too. I sat up and rubbed my eyes. Perhaps nearly falling asleep in a music lesson wasn't the best way to repay the nuns.

I yawned behind my hand and thought back to my conversation with the station master. There were so many loose ends swirling round my head, it was quite exhausting.

Standing up, I clapped my hands.

"Girls! Pack up all your things now; homework is to finish off writing the words of your carol – and to make a start on composing the melody and chords. We continue later in the week. See you then!"

I took the stairs two at a time to Slum Alley, slowing down to a brisk walk on the top landing when I heard footsteps. Running in the corridors was strictly forbidden at St Cecilia's and although this didn't mean that no one did it, as a member of staff I supposed I should try, at least occasionally, to set a good example.

Once in my room, I flung open the cupboard. I had remembered something significant. Ferreting around in my travel grip, I found last year's birthday present from my parents – my missing gloves! I remembered shoving them deep inside the side compartment as I had gathered my belongings in a hurry and leapt from the train yesterday. Thank goodness! I sat on my bed and cradled them, inhaling their special earthy fragrance.

Hang on! There was something else in my mind competing for my attention. Another loose end. Oh, my head hurt so much. Perhaps I should find an aspirin...no, wait a minute. What had the station master collected in his lost property box apart from the book, the cheese sandwich and the crochet needle? No, it was a knitting needle. I clutched my sore head; this was like that game we always played at Christmas where you had a tray of objects and then it was covered with a tea towel and you had to see how many you could name. A real test of memory. Ah ha! I knew what it was. The station master had found a strange metallic button.

A memory swam into my mind – a vision of Sister Claire standing in the Entrance Hall downstairs looking dishevelled with a button missing from her outdoor cape. My pulse quickened. How had she come to lose that button? And more importantly, why had she taken so long to arrive at St Cecilia's when she had been on the same train as me?

What on earth was going on?

Chapter 5

"It's the button, you see, that alerted me," I said. "Don't you think it's weird? And her habit looked so short that I could see her ankles and nuns don't usually display their ankles, do they? She's taller than she should be. Older too! The light in the corridor illuminated all her wrinkles..."

"Flora, please! Calm down!" Reverend Mother steered me towards the sofa.

Five minutes ago I had knocked on the door of the Nuns' Quarters, begging to speak to her. She had taken one look at me, then taken me to the Blue Parlour.

"You're nearly hysterical! Take a deep breath, that's it."

I filled my lungs, then started again.

"The way she pronounced choir – with a definite 'r' – it isn't normal. Unless you're not English. She sounds as if she's from across the pond..."

"Across the pond?" Reverend Mother's eyebrows squiggled upwards.

"America. It's what people say, not important, but what does concern me, is how much do you really know about her?"

"As much as I need to," Reverend Mother said. "She wrote a charming letter asking if she could come and stay for a while and I certainly know the Reverend Mother in her convent very well, and am confident she gave Sister Claire her blessing to come over. I'm not completely sure why you're asking all these questions, Flora dear."

"Well, it's because, because, oh, and I know this sounds mad, but I don't actually think she is Sister Claire. She's not like the lady I saw on the train, in so many ways..."

Reverend Mother threw her head back and let out a real belly laugh, then stopped when she saw my face.

"Oh, sorry Flora, but this is simply absurd! I've just been talking to Sister Claire and we've been discussing the sights of Rome – the Spanish Steps, the Coliseum and so on. How could she know all about that if she's not Sister Claire and hasn't been living in Italy for years? And why does it matter that a button's fallen off her habit?"

"But Reverend Mother," I began, "don't you see how easy it would be to look up a few details about Rome? Anyone could do that. There's probably information in our library upstairs. And as for the button, I don't know why it's important, I just have a feeling – a bad one."

"But what would be the point?" Reverend Mother said. "I mean of pretending to be someone else?"

She patted my arm and I felt tears welling up.

"Tell you what, I think a nice cup of tea is in order. Is your headache still bothering you? I'll bring an aspirin with the tea tray. Don't you move! Sit still – or better still, have a tiny lie down."

She swept away and I lay back on the sofa and rubbed my aching temples. I did feel rather wretched.

Within minutes she appeared again, with the headmistress trotting along behind, carrying a large tray.

"I've asked Sister Barbara to join us," Reverend Mother said. "I hope you don't mind but I have shared a few of your concerns with her."

Sister Barbara sat down very close to me. "Do you remember last year, my dear," she said gently, "when you had your, ahem, your Trouble?"

Was I likely to forget Charles the Rat dumping me for one of my best friends?

I nodded.

"And do you remember," Reverend Mother said, "how you got a few things out of proportion, thinking some of the girls were laughing at you and worried at one of the concerts that the parents would be staring at you to see if you'd been crying?"

"If you mean do I remember getting rather paranoid and thinking everyone was talking about me all the time, then yes," I admitted. "I certainly do!"

Even though everyone actually had been talking about me constantly, and noticing the white band of skin on my ring finger where my missing engagement ring had once been.

There had been one dreadful occasion when I'd overheard two girls in a lesson having a whispered conversation.

"Do you think she did something wrong, for her fiancé to have left her?" one girl had said.

"No, it won't be her fault; it's always the man, that's what my mum says..." the other replied.

"So what do you think happened?"

"I expect he met someone more glamorous."

"That's mean! Miss Gold is very pretty."

"Pretty, yes, but not glamorous, like a film star."

"No, I suppose not..."

They had carried on in this thoughtless way for ages, completely oblivious to the fact that I could hear them.

Recollecting their conversation now as I sat in the Blue Parlour tipped me right over the edge. The dam of my tears burst its bank. Sister Barbara took me in her motherly arms and I sat there sobbing for quite a while, the two nuns comforting me as best they could.

"He wasn't the right one for you, Flora," Reverend Mother said.

"Plenty more fish in the sea," Sister Barbara said.

"Is there anyone you want us to call – Susie perhaps? She might be better equipped to deal with affairs of the heart."

I shook my head and then blew my nose vigorously.

"I'm fine. Just tired – didn't sleep well last night."

"Maybe you're getting a touch of flu?" Sister Barbara said.

"Drink your tea and take the aspirin." Reverend Mother held out the white tablet and I swigged it down with a lukewarm mouthful of Lapsang.

"Biscuit?" Sister Barbara held out a china plate lined with a lace doily and I chose a custard cream.

"Have another," she urged. "You need feeding up."

I took a squashed fly Garibaldi biscuit and then, after further encouragement, a chocolate finger.

Five minutes later I was feeling both much better, and also like a prize idiot. How could I have made such a fuss about a visitor to the convent that I knew next to nothing about? Who did I think I was – Miss Marple?

It was all because I was still upset over Charles – I knew that now. I still had a long way to go before I could forget him and recover.

"Early night," Reverend Mother said as she stacked the tray.

"Have a nice hot bath first," Sister Barbara said, producing a large bottle of Badedas from a deep pocket in the folds of her habit. "I always find this so relaxing."

I'd long ago given up being surprised by some of the things the nuns did or said.

"Thank you – both of you." I sniffed. "I feel so much better."

I said goodnight to my two guardian angels at the foot of the stairs and then made my way up to

Slum Alley.

Ten minutes later I was covered in scented bubbles and lying in lukewarm water, my thoughts drifting. It was kind of Sister Barbara to suggest a hot bath, but she must have been aware that the school boiler would fail to provide any water of a temperature above tepid at this hour. I appreciated the intention, though.

I hadn't got into a state like this for ages and ages. Mostly, any thoughts of Charles were firmly shut away in a locked box at the back of my mind, although I'd had that wobble on the train coming back to school yesterday.

No point in dwelling on it, as my mother was fond of saying. Her other words of wisdom included, 'It is what it is', 'All will be well', and her all-time favourite, 'Let's draw a line under it'. I sighed heavily and several bubbles leapt into the air from the bath water, making me smile.

Once back in my room, I hopped into bed and tried to distract myself with a novel. This was better. Gosh, Jane Eyre did attend a really terrible school, didn't she? The girls at St Cecilia's didn't know how lucky they were.

My eyelids closed and I could feel myself drifting away.

Suddenly, I heard a door slam outside in the corridor. Probably one of the other staff coming up to their room. Must be late by now. There were only eight resident staff, all of us housed in Slum Alley, and all of us young unmarried women. No men were allowed to live in, of course; that would have worried the nuns far too much. The rest of the staff either lived out in the nearby towns and villages, like Susie, or were nuns and so lived downstairs on the floor below, in the Nun's Quarters.

All the pupils were incredibly curious about how the nuns lived; last term an intrepid girl had dared to sneak into a nun's bedroom. She managed to have a good snoop around and later, had been overheard chatting to her friends about what she had seen. This had caused vast amusement amongst all the staff – especially the nuns.

The conversation had run something like this:

"What was the nun's bedroom like?"

"Very small – not much in it."

"Not even a bed?"

"Of course a bed, and a wardrobe and a chest of drawers."

"A mirror? Did she have a mirror?"

"No mirror. But a table by the bed with a book on."

"What was it – the Lives of the Saints?"

"No – a Latin text book. Probably preparing our lesson for the next day."

"Nothing else? Nothing forbidden?"

"Like what?"

"Oh, I don't know...a whisky bottle? Magazine? Bag of sweets?"

"Not that I could see – but I didn't look in the wardrobe."

"Why not?"

"Because I could hear footsteps and legged it!"

I smiled at the memory, put my book on the side and switched off the light. A few tears threatened, but I gave myself a stern talking to and soon drifted off to sleep.

When I awoke, it was still dark outside. Looking at my folding alarm clock, I could see from the illuminated dial that it was barely six o'clock. I jerked my head towards the door when I thought I heard footsteps directly outside my room.

What would anyone be doing out there? My room was at the end of the corridor, so there was no need for anyone to pass by.

Shivering, I crept out of bed in my nightie. All quiet. I waited a few moments then flung the door open – in time to see the end of a veil whisking round the corner in the dim light.

I couldn't sleep after that; all my suspicious thoughts about Sister Claire came thrusting back at me like daggers, causing my head to throb painfully. Eventually I padded next door to the tiny kitchen to put the kettle on for an early morning cuppa. Looking out of the window, I could see the sun breaking through with the promise of a bright autumnal day. And Joe would be arriving this morning for his first day as the new violin teacher.

My heart began to hum the tune it had started when I'd first seen him in the Entrance Hall on Sunday. It managed to get to the second line of the melody this time.

I opened the metal casement window, longing to feel fresh air on my face. Far below, a black clad figure moved swiftly across the drive and disappeared round the back of the Hall. Who would be out walking at this hour of the morning? Most of the nuns would be praying in their rooms, getting ready for Chapel. And why would they be taking the path behind the Hall – when the only place it led to was the Music Hut?

Chapter 6

Before Assembly that same morning, I nipped down to the Hut, taking the route through the Undercroft rather than the outside path as it had started to rain a little.

"Oh, hi Susie!" I said, nearly bumping into her in the gloom.

She was mopping the floor in the corner.

"Reverend Mother's working you too hard," I said. "You should be having a coffee in the Staff Room, not busy down here."

She laughed. "Reverend Mother didn't ask me to do this," she said. "I like to keep the Undercroft floor clean, even if the rest of the area is a bit neglected. It's peaceful down here early in the morning. Brings back memories of when I first worked here. Anyway, what about you? You're not sipping coffee in the Staff Room either. You're a fine one to talk – always whizzing about. Don't think you know what the word relax means."

"Oh, I needed to pick up my hymn book and I also wanted to make sure Joe's teaching room was tidy – it wouldn't do if he didn't feel welcome on his first day."

I sped on until I reached the Hut. As I put the key in the lock, I noticed a slight mark on the paintwork. Strange!

Once inside, I walked through to the smaller room which was used for instrumental lessons.

"Phew! All fine here – I can see the nuns have been busy hoovering and the piano seems to be shinier than ever."

I sniffed the beeswax fragrance appreciatively, knowing I would forever associate it with St Cecilia's. That, and the less welcome smell of damp hockey socks lingering in the corridors...

Back in the Hall, I sorted out my music, marking the hymn numbers for Assembly with little bits of paper. Very soon, a stampede of girls arrived from all directions and lined up in a massive horseshoe shape.

"Hymn books open, girls!" Sister Barbara said. "And Miss Gold, if you please..."

I played the introduction to *All things bright and beautiful*, and then hundreds of young voices rose up to the rafters.

"The sunset and the morning that brightens up the sky..."

My fingers grasped at the chords of the accompaniment on the piano and I felt my spirits rise too. This was going to be a good day! Joe would be arriving soon – his first pupil was timetabled for ten o'clock, and as I had a free lesson first thing, that meant I could offer him a coffee in the Staff Room first...

All at once my fingers slipped onto an excruciatingly painful discord and I heard a cheeky girl giggling nearby. Crumbs! I needed to concentrate.

"And now, girls," Sister Barbara said, "I have an announcement before you go to class. Mr Oak will be joining us today – his first day at St Cecilia's as our new violin teacher, and I do hope you will be welcoming and polite if you see him in the corridor."

There was a slight disturbance at that point, with many girls becoming hysterical at the mere thought of a new male on the premises. Then I heard the cheeky girl near me whispering to her neighbour.

"I used to learn with the last violin teacher – he was useless. Wonder if this one's any better?"

"Doubt it," her neighbour said. "We saw him when he came for his interview, when we were running about on the Nun's Lawn. Saw him through the French windows. All smiles when he was drinking his tea with Miss Gold and Reverend Mother, but he won't last five minutes when he takes orchestra, you mark my words."

I immediately resolved to make sure I was around for the first orchestra rehearsal. The girls would not be given the opportunity to make mincemeat of Joe. Not on my watch.

"Miss Gold!" Sister Barbara's voice broke into my reverie. "The next hymn, if you please."

"Oh, yes, so sorry, dear me." I picked up the hymn book but before I could find the right page, I dropped it on the floor, scattering the markers far and wide.

"Here you are, Miss Gold," a helpful pupil said, passing me the book.

"Number 535," Sister Barbara said, saving the situation, and I played the introduction. The school collectively breathed in and my hands were poised over the keyboard to launch into the first verse when a piecing whisper echoed round the Hall.

"A car! There's a car coming up the drive!"

All the girls' heads swivelled to the bay window facing the drive.

Sister Barbara clapped her hands. "Girls! Girls! Pay attention please. Look this way!"

No one appeared to hear this command, but continued gawping; I joined in and saw Joe stepping out of a red Mini parked at a rakish angle next to the front door.

Heavens! I had forgotten to explain to him at his interview the necessity of parking round the side in the staff car park. Reverend Mother was very hot on keeping the drive looking tidy and she wouldn't be at all amused. Oops, there she was now, coming out of the front door. Surprisingly, she looked very pleased to see Joe, not the slightest bit cross, and was holding her hand out to him.

"He's wearing a tan corduroy jacket," one of the girls said.

"Yes, and he's got ankle boots on."

"He's not bald, like the last violin teacher."

"I want to learn the violin! Do you think I should ring my parents tonight and ask?"

"Girls!" Sister Barbara's voice rose an octave. "We are going to sing this hymn, so I suggest you face this way immediately so that we can begin, or we will still be here at teatime. Miss Gold – would you mind playing the introduction again?"

Over coffee in the staffroom, I described the whole incident to Joe, struggling to give the full details as I was cackling so much.

"Cripes!" he said. "I did have a weird feeling I was being spied on, but I didn't realise the entire school were scrutinising me."

"Well they were," I said.

Including the staff.

"Now you've got a taste of what a goldfish must feel like."

"Yes," he agreed, "in a very small bowl. Seriously though, you will be around when I give my first lesson, won't you? In case I need help?"

"You won't need my help," I said, "but yes, I'll be next door in the main part of the Hut if there's an emergency."

"We could have a sort of code," Joe suggested. "If I feel it's all getting too much, I could ask you for another music stand; then you'd know you need to come and rescue me."

"Could work," I said, "unless you really did need another music stand. That would be awkward, wouldn't it?"

Joe gave a broad grin and his eyes crinkled attractively. I sobered up a little and tried to slow the rhythm of my heart. This wouldn't do. Had I already forgotten again about vowing to keep my distance?

Reverend Mother came into the Staff Room and beamed when she saw Joe.

"All going well?" she asked him. "Is Flora looking after you all right?"

"I'm so sorry I forget to tell Joe, I mean Mr Oak, about the staff car park," I said. "I realise you don't want staff cars on the drive because they look untidy."

Reverend Mother threw her hands in the air. "Heavens! I don't mind Joe parking there! He's a creative person – I think the rules are different for him, and besides, his car is so sweet, isn't it? I do love Minis."

She swept out of the room, leaving me open mouthed, while several other staff members sniggered.

"Special treatment already and you haven't even given one lesson yet," I said. "Still, at least she's not cross with me for forgetting to tell you about the parking."

Joe glanced at his watch. "Talking of my car, I need to go and collect my violin from the boot before the first lesson."

"Yes, you do that," I said. "I'll be along in a minute – just need to finish my coffee."

Once he'd gone, I picked up the local paper that

was lying on the side and began reading the headlines.

Dog Show a great success...Parish Council to meet and discuss the new bypass...Lady in hospital does not know...

"That new bypass will be useful," Susie said, looking over my shoulder. "It'll cut quite a bit of time off my commute."

"Oh hi, Susie," I said. "Didn't see you come in."

"No," she said. "You were quite wrapped up in Mr Joe Oak. He is rather handsome, I must say."

I blushed.

"Is he single?" she asked.

"I don't know," I said. "And I have no interest in that anyway – you know I'm off men."

Susie sat down beside me. "Time that wasn't the case," she said. "Time you got back in the ring. He might be the one for you and you don't want to miss out, do you?"

"Heavens!" I said. "I'll be late if I don't run. The Upper 3s will be on their way down to music by now."

"See you at choir this evening," Susie called.

"Oh yes!" I said. "I must remember to tell Joe about it. I hope he wants to join – the more the merrier."

I dashed along the corridor and managed to get to the Hut in time to stop the hordes of girls charging in.

"Line up please girls, that's it. Now, as we go in, I want you to be very quiet as there is an instrumental lesson already in progress – yes, that's right, it's the new violin teacher. Quieten down girls! That's it. Like mice, please, as we go in."

I turned round and glared when I heard someone squeaking like a demented rodent, but very soon all was quiet and we were able to start the lesson and continue working on their Christmas compositions. While I wandered from group to group, listening to their ideas, I could hear the sweet comforting tone of Joe's violin in the background as he demonstrated pieces to his pupils.

After a very busy day, it was time for choir.

"Hello, ladies and gentlemen!" I said, standing in front of an impressively large crowd.

The rehearsal was for girls and any local parents or staff who wanted to join in. This evening I was thrilled to spot the taxi driver and his wife among the rows of singers in the Hall.

"Welcome to the run up to Christmas. We've got a matter of weeks to get the choral items ready for the big Christmas Carol Concert and I'm sure you're raring to go, so we're going to kick off with some exercises. On your feet please. That's it!"

I sat down at the piano and bashed out a few chords, then we all started our vocal warm-ups.

"Ahhhhhh, Ayyyyyy, Eeeeeee..."

"Beautiful! Now, please pass these copies out..."

I made a valiant attempt not to keep looking at the basses where Joe was sitting, but kept finding my eye drawn that way. No! I simply had to look somewhere else...at the sopranos for instance. Ah! The nuns were out in force this evening, excellent. And they were swelling the altos too.

My mouth went dry. Sister Claire was sitting in the altos, head down, crouched over her music. She was a very intense woman. Had she been outside my door early this morning? Was she also the mysterious figure I'd seen out of the window? Perhaps she'd been on her way to the Music Hut. Did she wish me harm?

I stood up straight and tried to concentrate on the music. I had absolutely no evidence of any wrong doing. Except there was a mark on the door of the Music Hut and I had seen a veil whisking away early this morning near my room...but no, it was too ridiculous. I was being paranoid. Again.

During the break, the nuns served tea and biscuits and I wandered over to chat to the taxi driver. "Thank you for coming. How are you finding the rehearsal?"

"Great," he said. "I'd forgotten how much better I feel after a good sing – my wife's having a ball, too," he said, indicating a kindly looking lady standing with some other altos. He took an appreciative slurp of his tea. "Who's that lady, talking to my wife? The nun?"

"Oh, that's Sister Claire. She arrived on Sunday – she was on the same train as I was. Do you remember that I asked you if you'd seen her coming out of the station? You saw her leaving with another lady."

"That's not the nun I saw on Sunday," he said slowly. "I've a good memory for faces – on account of being in the police for many years. That's certainly not the nun who came out of the station. I have seen her before, though."

"Have you?" I asked. "Where?"

I could feel my heart racing, and not in a pleasant way.

"If I'm not very much mistaken," he said, rocking back on his heels, "she's the lady the nun was talking to. The lady who took the nun by the arm and led her round to the side of the station. So how come she's dressed as a nun herself now?"

Chapter 7

I have no idea how I got through the rest of the rehearsal that evening. Images of nuns' faces billowed around my head, together with missing buttons, creaking floorboards, scuff marks on paintwork and Sister Claire's ankles in her too short habit. Or were they someone else's ankles?

Who would I be able to turn to with my questions? Sister Barbara and Reverend Mother wouldn't be inclined to take me seriously after my meltdown the day before. I could try talking to the taxi driver again at the end of the rehearsal; he had been a policeman, after all. Maybe he would either put my mind at rest – that would be a relief – or report to his former colleagues in the police station if he thought there was something criminal going on.

As I crashed down onto the last chord and the choir sang their final 'Jah!' of 'Hallelujah!' I jumped to my feet.

"Thank you so much everyone! A splendid rehearsal, absolutely terrific. So much potential. Now, don't forget you're very welcome to take the music home and do a spot of private practice – few little corners need sorting for some of you – and I'll see you all at the same time next week."

I managed to waylay the taxi driver as he was leaving.

"You know what you said, about thinking the nun you saw at the station on Sunday didn't look the same as the nun here tonight, in fact the nun here looks like the lady you saw with the nun – if you get my meaning?"

The taxi driver nodded, while his wife blinked rapidly.

"Oh yes," he said. "I remember."

He looked across at Sister Claire who was folding sheets of Christmas music and stuffing them into her pocket.

At least someone was taking me at my word and intending to do some practice before the next rehearsal.

Screwing his eyes up, the taxi driver continued, "Although, now I take another look, I'm not so sure."

His wife laughed. "That's because you forgot your glasses this evening," she said. "Left them in the car I expect. It's getting to be a habit! I'm surprised you could read any of the music."

"To be honest," the taxi driver admitted, "it was an uphill battle, especially with these lights. Half of them don't seem to work."

I followed his gaze upwards to the vast metal chandelier in the centre of the Hall, lit by a few feeble bulbs shaped like candles.

"Hello," Joe said, as he joined our group. "I say – do you have the usual tradition after choir practice in this neck of the woods."

"What's that?" the taxi driver's wife asked.

"An outing to the pub," Joe said.

"Not for us, but maybe another time," the taxi driver said. "Early start tomorrow with an airport run."

"See you next week," his wife said.

"Goodbye and thanks for coming," I said. "And sorry, Joe – I don't usually go the pub after choir, makes me too tired for work the next day, but I could manage a cup of tea in the Staff Room if you're interested."

"Great idea," Joe said. He turned and clicked his fingers; instantly a couple of girls came running over.

"Yes Mr Oak? How may we help?"

"Would you mind awfully picking up all the bits of music from around the room," he said. "It would help Miss Gold – and me."

"Of course, Mr Oak."

"Anything for you, Mr Oak."

"We'd love to!"

Very soon we set off to the Staff Room, leaving Joe's fans to clear up.

"It usually takes me ages to tidy the Hall after a rehearsal," I said. "It's quite unbelievable how many people plonk their music down anywhere after singing – and I'm not only talking about the girls."

As I opened the Staff Room door, I saw Sister Claire sitting on the sofa; her legs were crossed and she was totally absorbed in the local newspaper. She jumped to her feet as soon as she saw us and rushed away, the paper flying onto the floor and the door banging noisily behind her.

"Something we said?" Joe asked.

"Don't joke," I said. "There's something very odd about that woman."

"In what way?"

I bit my lip and reached for the kettle. "Not entirely sure. But something's not right."

Over tea, I found myself confiding in Joe about all the strange suspicions I'd had about Sister Claire.

"Probably sounds bonkers to you," I said with a nervous laugh. "My mother always says I'm too nosy for my own good."

"It doesn't sound bonkers," Joe said. "More intriguing."

He took a sip of tea. "I've always been inquisitive too. When I was a little boy, I wanted to be a detective – not a police detective, more of a Hercule Poirot sort of figure. Turned out there were more openings for violin teachers than private investigators, so here I am."

"You're very welcome," I said.

He really did have the most gorgeous eyes and I was beginning to forget all about my intention to be strictly professional as I felt my insides melting...

"Any chance of a biscuit?" Joe asked. "I'm a bit peckish."

I jumped up. "I'll have a rummage in the cupboard and see what I can find."

"Quite fancy a squashed fly," Joe said.

"Ah! The nuns' favourites."

As I wrestled with the dented lid of the biscuit tin, I could hear the crinkly sound of a newspaper being unfolded.

"Let's find out what Sister Claire was so fascinated in," Joe said.

"There's nothing in that rag," I said. "I had a quick glance earlier. Dog show, new bypass – oh, and an article about a lady in hospital. All riveting stuff!"

"Nevertheless, I'm going to take a look. Ok, I'll start with the bypass...ah, see what you mean. This is fairly technical and dull...what about the dog show? Do you like dogs?"

"Allergic to them," I said.

"Shame," he said. "I'd like to get a dog one day, when I'm settled."

Did he mean when he was married with a family? Did he want to get married? Was he thinking of settling down? Could he mean...?

"But a dog ties you down, doesn't it?" Joe continued. "I don't want any of that at the moment. Footloose and fancy free, that's me! Now, lady in hospital...where is it, ah! Success!"

Joe read the article out loud in a clear commanding voice.

"Lady in hospital after losing her memory. Concern is growing as to the identity of a person found in a wood late on Sunday afternoon. She was found by a local dog walker in a confused state, clutching a string of rosary beads, claiming she'd been tied up in a cottage after being kidnapped..."

I spun round, my Miss Marple antennae on high alert.

"I say!" Joe sprang to his feet, a half-eaten squashed fly biscuit dropping to the ground. "I rather wish I had the little grey cells of Hercule Poirot, because this is adding up to something mighty suspicious. You don't think..."

"Yes," I said. "I do! I think our Sister Claire is an imposter. I can't brush away the evidence any longer. Now, where did they say this mysterious woman has been taken? Which hospital?"

Within minutes, Joe and I were shooting down the drive in his Mini, on our way to town.

I watched the manly sinews in his hands rippling as he masterfully steered the car round sharp bends at fearsome speeds. He screeched to a halt outside the hospital.

"What are we going to do next?" I asked.

"Not sure," he said. "Presume it's too late for visiting hour?"

"Yes, definitely," I said. "That means that Sister Claire – if the lady who's lost her memory is the real Sister Claire – is safe for now."

"Do you think they will have a police presence at her bedside?" Joe asked.

"Don't think so," I replied. "I expect her story about being kidnapped hasn't been taken too seriously. What do you think?"

"Probably right," Joe said.

"We could go into the reception and ask if we could use the phone to ring the police," I suggested.

"And say what?"

"Say that we've just seen the imposter Sister Claire arriving in a taxi and careering up the steps of the hospital," I yelled, opening the car door. "And we think she's up to no good!"

"Crikey!" Joe said as we ran into the building hot on the heels of Sister Claire's imposter.

"Which ward for the lady who's lost her memory?" I begged.

The receptionist glared at me. "Visiting hours are over! You can't barge in here whenever you feel like it."

"Has someone been in asking the same thing?" I said. "Please, as quick as you can, it's so important."

"I'm not at liberty to say."

"It's a matter of life and death!" Joe said. "Possibly."

The receptionist pursed her lips "Well, if that's the case, we do have a lady upstairs in the condition you mention, but I still can't let you visit her as she's got someone with her at the moment."

"But you said no visitors," I pointed out, "so why have you let someone in to see her?"

"Ah, but that was a special case. She's a nun from the convent. I went to a convent school and I know

Ordinary Rules don't apply to Holy People."

"Call the police!" I bellowed as we made for the stairs.

Finally the receptionist seemed to get our drift because she shouted after us, "Second floor! Ward 3. Bed at the end..."

We raced into Ward 3, nearly falling over on the slippery floor. Several startled patients looked up; it must have been the most exciting thing that had happened for a long while.

A nurse ran after us, bleating, "You can't come in here like this! Stop! I'll have to call security!"

"Call away!" I screamed. "Please! Do anything you want, only don't get in our way."

Eventually we reached the end of the ward and were met with billowing pink curtains.

Joe flung them aside to reveal a lady asleep in the bed. Sister Claire was leaning over her, clutching a pillow.

Chapter 8

The lady with the pillow – who I knew now for certain wasn't Sister Claire – shot past us and pushed open the fire escape door, disappearing just before a policemen pounded down the ward.

"Where am I?" Sister Claire asked from her bed. "What's going on?" She sat up. "I've been having the funniest dream...I seem to have been caught in a whirlwind...oh!" She stared at me. "Don't I know you? Have we met?"

"Not exactly," I said. "But I saw you on a train on Sunday."

She hit her hand against her forehead. "Of course! The train. You were there in the carriage when I got on. It was very full, wasn't it? And that kind man gave up his seat for me. It's so good to know there are still gentleman around."

"Do you know who you are?" Joe asked

"Who I am?" She wrinkled up her forehead. "Of course I do, what a silly question. I'm Sister Claire. Why do you ask?"

She looked around the ward, a puzzled expression on her face. "Have I been ill?"

"I think we'd better leave Sister Claire to be

looked after by the nurses," the policeman said, looking at me and Joe. "If you wouldn't mind coming outside, we need to have a chat."

"But officer," I said. "You need to find Sister Claire – I mean the nun who has just run away. It's top priority."

"Sister Claire is right here," the policeman said.

"Yes," she said, attempting to get out of bed. "I most certainly am."

The nurse pulled the covers over her again. "There, there; you need to rest."

"No, I don't," she insisted. "I've remembered an awful lot. Not everything, but every minute a few more pieces of the jigsaw are slotting into place. And one thing I know for certain, you need to get after the lady who was here a minute ago as fast as you can. She's the one who kidnapped me and left me tied up in a cottage. Seems to have stolen my habit as well. She forced me to wear her clothes, which were much too big. I must say, though, this hospital gown is very cosy. Nice colour too. I've always liked green."

My eyes met Joe's and I knew he was thinking the same thing; at last, the mystery was beginning to untangle.

"I know I've come over from Rome to stay at St Cecilia's," Sister Claire said, "but I can't quite remember why. Yet. But I do remember that unpleasant lady who has just run off. She came up to me on my way out of Gillingham Station on Sunday. Nice as pie she was in the beginning, asking me if

I was on my way to the convent, and saying she'd been sent to collect me. I thought I'd be getting a taxi, but she said she'd whizz me to St Cecilia's in no time in her car."

"What happened next?" Joe asked.

"She took me round to the side of the station and shoved me inside her car so fast, my cape got caught in the door and a button flew off. I wanted to look for it but she said we didn't have time. She drove me to a cottage in the middle of nowhere, and I remember..."

The policeman held up his hand for quiet as a call came through on his radio.

"I see..." Then he shook his head.

"Bad news," he said to us. "Officers at the bottom of the fire escape gave chase but the lady got clean away. They said she moved spectacularly fast, particularly for a nun."

"She's not a nun!" I said.

"Mmm..." The policeman put his head on one side. "I think you'd better tell me everything you know."

The patients in the nearby beds leant forwards; this was much more invigorating than listening to hospital radio or reading their books.

"Fire away!" the policeman said.

Joe and I started babbling at the same time.

"Missing button..."

"Her habit was too short..."

"She seemed to have a sore throat but when I'd heard her on the train, her voice had been clear..."

"So many little clues that she wasn't who she said she was...wrinkles..."

The policeman shook his head. "Let's try it another way." He looked at Sister Claire. "Had you seen the woman who kidnapped you before?"

"No," she said, "well, as far as I can remember...and why anyone would want to kidnap me is beyond me. I don't have an enemy in the world – as far as I know. Unless...oh, I feel rather odd..."

"Miss Gold?" the policeman said. "Anything to add?"

"There's one important detail I haven't told you yet, officer," I said. "This woman pronounced 'choir' in a very odd way."

"Is this relevant?" the policeman said.

"Oh yes! Because, you see, she pronounced the 'r' in choir like an American might, but the rest of the time she talked carefully and slowly."

The policeman scratched his head.

"As if she was trying to suppress an accent," I explained. "I think she's American. That might be a clue."

"It's all coming back to me," Sister Claire said, "and I think I know who she is. Grace. I've known about her for some time, but hadn't come across her in the flesh until she accosted me outside the station." Sister Claire frowned deeply. "I might of course be mistaken and I do still feel a tiny bit confused – but if I'm right, then I feel sorry for her. Because she is a lady in pain."

"You were reading a book about America on the

train," I said. "Is there some sort of connection with this Grace?"

"Fancy you noticing my book," Sister Claire said. "You are terribly observant."

"What's the link?" Joe asked. "Between the American accent and you being interested in America?"

Sister Claire plucked at the sheets of her bed. "I can't say. Not until I've spoken to, well, to someone very important. It will be too much of a shock for her otherwise."

"Can't say?" The policeman stamped his foot on the ground. "Or won't say? Sister, this is important. My officers are looking for a kidnapper. If there are any clues, however small, you need to share them now."

Tears rolled down Sister Claire's face and the nurse beside her put her arm round her.

"That's enough now," the nurse said. "This line of questioning might be helping you but it isn't doing my patient any good and she's my top priority. I don't want her upset further."

She helped Sister Claire to lie down again and smoothed the sheets over her. "There, you have a little snooze – don't you worry about a thing."

The nurse practically manhandled all of us out of the cubicle and there was a disappointed sigh from the bed-ridden spectators all around. Drawing the pink curtain, the nurse turned to face us. "I know your investigation is important, officer," she said, "but my patient has only recently recovered her memory, in fact it only seems a partial recall to me, and she's in a very delicate state. Maybe come back in the morning?"

The policeman inclined his head. We followed him downstairs and as we stood in the Entrance Hall he said, "I'll be in touch with you – we'll probably need to have another chat."

"Of course, Officer," Joe said. "Anything we can do to help."

"But what if Grace returns?" I asked.

"Don't you worry out that," the policeman said. "I'm staying here at the hospital; no one's going to get past me."

Joe gave me a lift back to the convent in his Mini.

"What a day!" I said as we swept up the drive.

"Yes!" he said. "I can't believe so much has happened on my first teaching day at St Cecilia's. It seems an age ago I was giving my first violin lesson in the Music Hut."

"Then choir practice as well today," I said, "and the mad dash to the hospital. A real baptism of fire!"

"I wonder if the police have rung Reverend Mother," Joe said. "Or whether they expect us to let her know the news?"

"Not sure," I said. "The nuns tend not to answer the phone this late in the evening. I could go to the Nuns' Quarters and let them know."

"What could they do about anything at this hour, except worry?" Joe said. "No, leave them be."

"But what if Grace comes back to the convent?" I

said.

"She'll be as far away from here as possible by now," Joe said. "She wouldn't dare show her face again at St Cecilia's. She'd be too frightened the police would be here."

"Perhaps they should be here?"

Joe put his hand on my leg for an instant before changing gear. "Don't worry; it will all be fine."

I couldn't say anything at all for a few moments after that; my heart was definitely singing now, not merely humming. Singing a very hopeful tune.

We reached the top of the drive and I stepped out. "Thank you so much for the lift."

"Pleasure! See you tomorrow bright and early. My second day at St Cecilia's!"

I waved and set off round the back of the Hall as he swung the car round in a circle to face down the drive. Stopping, he wound the window down.

"Hey! Thought you'd be turning in," he said. "Don't tell me you're going to the Music Hut?"

I rubbed my eyes. "Yes; I have a few things to tidy up for the morning. The girls who cleared the Hall for us after choir will have dumped the music all over the place in my room and it will save time in the morning if I sort it out now."

"You don't want to be doing that," Joe said. "I can help you tidy up in the morning. Be off with you to bed!"

"No, it's fine." I said. "I'd prefer to get it done right away. That's how I am – I worry about things and find the only way to put them out of my mind is to tackle them."

"Well, if you're sure – but don't be long," Joe said. "I'd like to think you'll be tucked up in bed by the time I get home."

With a cheery wave, he roared down the drive and I set off along the narrow outside path to the Hut. An owl hooted in the dark distance and the wind whistled and groaned through the trees in the woods.

Unlocking the door, I noticed the mark on the paint work again. Had Grace been responsible for this? A chill ran down my spine. And had it been her creeping round outside my room in the early hours?

It didn't take me long to tidy up. I was just putting the last sheet of music into a folder when I heard a voice behind me. A strong and confident drawl – an American accent.

"Think you're so clever, don't you? Well, Missy, let me tell you, I've had enough of your interference. If it hadn't been for you and your ridiculous boyfriend, I'd have managed to deal with that useless nun back there in the hospital. As it is, I'm on the run and Sister Claire is free to make all sorts of accusations against me."

I spun round; Grace was standing there in my Music Hut, glowering, her arm raised as if to strike me.

I attempted a shout for help but only a strangled whimper issued forth from my lips. Why hadn't I listened to Joe?

"I tried to deliver a warning note to you this morning," Grace snarled, "to tell you to keep your nose out. You've been far too interested in me from the very beginning."

"That was you?" I said. "Outside my room? And then – ah, I see! You tried to get in here..."

"But your precious Hut was locked," Grace said.

Suddenly she froze as Joe's voice was heard outside the Hut.

"Flora! Flora!" he called. "Are you all right?"

The curtains were closed – the nuns always insisted on this as they said it kept the heat in – and so Joe couldn't see that I had an unwelcome visitor with me, namely Grace the kidnapper.

She came over behind me and held me tightly. "Say there's nothing wrong." Was that a knife I could feel at my throat? I wasn't going to take any chances.

"I'm fine," I mumbled.

"Flora!" Joe said. "Open the door! I want to see if you're all right."

He rattled the door handle over and over.

"You didn't really think I wouldn't take the precaution of turning the key once I was inside, did you?" Grace hissed under her breath.

"Let me in!" Joe said. "I need to know you're OK."

How I wished he would just batter the door in!

"I'll harm Joe too, if you call out," Grace whispered. "Don't think you'd like that, would you?"

I gulped and croaked, "No!"

"Is there someone in there with you?" Joe asked.

"Persistent, isn't he?" Grace growled. "Tell you what, you're going to open the door, only a crack mind you, and speak to him. Don't try any funny business – because I'll know."

"What, what should I say?"

"Tell him you're alone and you're fine. You can add some stupid nonsense about your precious Music Department to make it realistic, then tell him to go home and that you shouldn't be on your own with him late at night. What would the nuns say? Not proper for a young woman like you. And I'll be right behind you the whole time."

"Coming," I said to Joe and staggered to the door with Grace holding my neck.

She loosened her grip once at the door but I could feel something hard pressing into my back.

"One false move!" she warned.

"Hello Joe," I stammered as I opened the door a tiny chink. "What are you doing here?"

"Thank goodness you're all right!" Joe said. "I was on my way down the drive when I thought I saw a bedraggled figure in the undergrowth by the side of the road so I decided to turn back to check you were OK. I should never have left you to make your way down here on your own."

"I'm fine," I said, blinking rapidly, desperately trying to give him a non-verbal signal.

"You look a bit tired," he said, "around the eyes."

The pressure in my back increased and I could feel Grace's hot breath on my neck.

Then I had an absolute corker of a brain wave.

What was it Joe and I had joked about that very morning? If he needed help when he was teaching, we would have a secret signal – he would ask me for something. Now, what was it? Ah yes!

"I need to find a music stand," I said. "It's very important that I have a music stand. Then I'll be fine and can get out of here and go up to my room."

"I understand," he said. "Well, goodnight and see you in the morning."

I closed the door and Grace pulled me across the room and shoved me onto a chair. "That wasn't so bad was it," she sneered.

"Stand back from the door!" came a shout and with a splintering explosion, the door literally flew off its hinges as Joe booted it in. What a hero!

"Flora, my darling!" Joe rushed over to me and folded me in his arms. "Are you all right?"

In the background I could hear the welcoming sound of a police siren and through the shattered door flocked quantities of anxious nuns clutching rosary beads.

Chapter 9

"You're not doing any teaching whatsoever this morning," Reverend Mother said firmly as she placed a rack of fresh toast on the table of the Staff Dining Room directly in front of me. "You are to put your feet up. Starting now."

"But Reverend Mother," I said, "I need to get on with the music for the concert...besides, who's going to teach my lessons?"

"I'm going to sit with your classes," Susie said. "Happy to help."

"What about Joe?" I asked. "Is he coming in to teach today?"

"He is," Reverend Mother said. "He absolutely insisted, said he didn't want to let the Music Department down – didn't want to let you down. What a brave man he is, don't you think?"

I didn't trust myself to answer. The welcome sound of Joe kicking the door in would stay with me for a long time. That, and the feeling of his strong arms around me.

I took an enormous bite of toast and thought for the umpteenth time how lucky I was that he had come back to rescue me.

"More coffee?" Susie asked.

"Thank you. You're all being very kind."

She sat down next to me. "I still don't understand how the police were there so quickly."

"Well," I said, "it turned out that Grace had been seen acting suspiciously by a member of the public not far from the end of the school drive and so the police had sent a patrol car up to the convent."

"Ah," she said, "that was lucky."

"And I was on the scene quickly, too," Reverend Mother said, "because I'd been woken earlier by the sound of Joe's Mini roaring back up the drive for a second time and so had roused the other members of the community; we were all very anxious to see what was going on. First we went outside to have a look at Joe's Mini, such an adorable car, and then we heard a shout from the Music Hut. We all rushed down there, praying like mad. The Good Lord definitely heard us, because when we got there, Joe was breaking the door down."

"It must have been a splendid sight, seeing Grace led away in handcuffs after what she'd put you through," Susie said to me.

"It was, but now, in the cold clear light of day, I feel sorry for her," I said. "She seemed quite deranged, so upset about something – no real idea what. She kept saying I'd meddled and made things difficult, blaming me for the fact that she'd been chased by the police."

"But it was her own actions that caused her to be on the run," Reverend Mother said.

"Yes," Susie said. "Don't forget, she kidnapped Sister Claire. And she seemed to be attempting a far worse crime there in the hospital."

"Who knows what would have happened if you and Joe hadn't discovered her next to Sister Claire's hospital bed?" Reverend Mother said.

This was true – but I felt in my bones that there was a bigger mystery still to be revealed. And when we knew what it was, it might shed some light on why Grace had behaved in this crazy fashion.

Reverend Mother patted my knee. "You did brilliantly! You managed to find the real Sister Claire – with Joe's help – and apparently, she'll be back here later today. I can't wait to meet her."

"So soon?" I asked. "I'm surprised the hospital are releasing her. She's been through quite an ordeal."

"So have you, my dear," Reverend Mother said. "Now, don't forget, no teaching this morning. I absolutely forbid it! I'll be bringing you a lovely big pile of magazines from the Nuns' Quarters to read – my cousin came straight over with them when she heard of your Troubles. And the biscuit tin has been replenished. You are absolutely forbidden to do anything whatsoever, except relax. I will be back to check on you later."

I had no doubt about that. She might have been a nun, but she had a pretty shrewd idea about human nature – in particular, mine. She knew full well that I was itching to get back to work – and that I wasn't above a bit of disobedience.

At first, I did as I had been told, and sat in the Staff Room with my feet up, chatting to passing staff who flitted in and out to collect books and snatch a quick coffee. I browsed the magazines and nibbled enough biscuits to feel that I might not deserve lunch. After a while, I became thoroughly bored and decided to go down to the Music Hut and see how Joe was getting on.

I sneaked out of a side door, rushing right down into the woods and round the long back way to the Music Department, anxious not to be seen by Reverend Mother as she would be bound to send me back to the Staff Room.

Once outside the Music Hut, I peered through the main window.

Susie was sitting at a table, beaming at the girls who were reclining in their chairs, some sadly glassy-eyed with boredom, but others lost in a musical day dream, while the sound of Beethoven burst forth from the box record player. Musical Appreciation – always kept the class quiet. If you followed it up with 'Why not draw a picture or write a poem inspired by what you've heard', you could earn yourself a double lesson of complete peace. I giggled as Susie noticed me peering in and wagged her finger at me.

Sneaking round to the other side of the Hut, I looked obliquely into the smaller room where Joe was teaching. A tiny junior girl was playing her violin while Joe accompanied on the piano. The gentle piano chords were at odds with the strange scraping sound of the miniature violin bow being dragged across the strings. The girl had a fluffy head of curls that shook as she sawed backwards and forwards, her tongue sticking out of the side of her mouth.

When the piece ended, Joe turned and beamed at her. I couldn't hear his words, but he was obviously pleased and appreciative of the little girl's efforts. He picked up his violin and began to draw the bow across a string very gently, then put his head on one side and looked up. He smiled at the girl and she tried the same thing with her violin; she was slowly taking her first steps along the path to developing a beautiful tone.

Very soon the girl was packing her instrument away and leaving the room with a spring in her step. I had to hand it to Joe, he was a born teacher; I predicted the number of girls learning violin was going to soar with him on the staff.

Unexpectedly, the window swung open and Joe called out, "I know you're there, Flora! I can see you reflected in the shiny piano case."

I stepped forward to face him. "Busted! And all because the nuns polish the pianos so much. If this was a normal school, there'd be so much dust and grime on that wood, you wouldn't have had a hope of seeing me mirrored there."

Joe smiled, his eyes flicking over my face. "How are you?"

"Fine!" I squeaked, sounding like a chipmunk.

Why did this always happen when I talked to him?

"Reverend Mother told me she was keeping you confined to the Staff Room with magazines and biscuits all morning – how did you escape? Why did you escape?"

"Well," I said, "as to how, that was easy, I just walked out. Although I was careful to take the long route through the woods, in case Reverend Mother had any of her spies on the lookout. And as for why, I'm surprised you have to ask that. How many magazine do you think I want to read about making casseroles and knitting matinee jackets?"

"None?"

"Too right! I want to get back to work, to get on with the preparations for the Carol Concert."

And I wanted to see Joe, my big strong rescuer, my...

He leant forwards, his arms on the window sill. "I dread to think what would have happened if I hadn't turned up. That woman, Grace, she's dangerous!"

"I know! I'm so grateful."

Then Joe plucked at his pullover, not meeting my eyes. "I, I think I probably said something foolish last night. I need to explain."

"Really?" My heart was beating like the bass drum in an orchestra. Loud, terrifying – and making you wonder what you're going to hear next.

"Yes." Joe looked straight at me. "I think I might have called you my darling, or some such nonsense."

He had! Oh joy! Now it was all going to begin. My heart was singing full throttle...

"Yes," he said. "That was it. I did call you my darling, but I want you to know that I didn't mean it, of course I didn't – it was said in the heat of the situation, that's all. I would never take advantage of you like that, try to make you feel you owed me something – it wouldn't be right, or proper..." His voice trailed off as the door to his room opened and a small person's head appeared.

"Mr Oak? Is this the right room? I think I'm supposed to be having my first violin lesson with you now."

"Come in, welcome." Joe gave me a cheerful wave and closed the window.

I turned and ran into the woods, not pausing until I was a considerable distance away from the scene of my dreadful disappointment, then promptly burst into floods of scalding tears.

He'd not only called me his darling last night, but he'd held me in his arms, where I'd felt safe and warm. Was that nothing? He hadn't meant it?

I wiped the sleeve of my jersey across my sodden face. It was my fault. I'd let my guard down. Hadn't I promised myself I wouldn't trust a man again, after Charles? It was bound to end in tears – in this case, before anything had properly started.

I walked along overgrown paths, feeling the cool breeze drying my face, caressing my swollen eyelids.

As I walked, I swung my arms and attempted a verse of *Once in Royal.* Hm, it would soon be time to get the choir to learn the descant for the last verse. My goodness, I had so much to get on with, to prepare for the Concert. It was going to be the best ever this year. And it was such a good thing that I had no romantic involvement to distract me – I was so pleased.

A tiny robin in the hedgerow put his head on one side, regarding me balefully.

"OK, Robin," I yelled. "I get it! You might think I'm kidding myself, but let me tell you, I don't want to have anything to do with Mr Joe Oak, beyond a strictly professional relationship, and that's the truth."

The robin twitched his head, said something like "Tic!" then flew away. He didn't seem to believe my protestations any more than I did.

What sort of man was Joe Oak anyway? Who did he think he was, hugging me one minute, calling me his darling, then doing a complete U-turn and saying it didn't mean anything?

My heart stopped trying to sing. It attempted a miserable pathetic little hum for a while, but by the time I was back in the Staff Room curled up over a magazine and a plate of custard creams, it had fallen entirely silent.

Chapter 10

The noise in the Refectory was deafening. I scooted over to the staff table with my plate of macaroni and sat at the opposite end to Joe.

"Quiet! Girls!" Reverend Mother screeched. "Ah! That's better! Now, I have an announcement. We will be having a visitor to the convent – she's arriving this afternoon and her name is Sister Claire."

"Wasn't that the name of the other nun?" a girl asked. "The American one?"

"Er, quite so," Reverend Mother said. "It was indeed. But this is the English Sister Claire."

"Has the other one left?" the girl asked.

"Yes, she has. Sadly. She found she was wanted elsewhere." Reverend Mother folded her arms.

Yes – wanted, as in wanted by the police.

"Is she coming back?" a girl asked.

"No. And no need to mention this in your letters home, is there?"

There was a frenzied whispering across the Refectory.

"Is there, girls? And did I mention there will be a super film this Sunday in the gym – for those who do as they're told?"

"No, Reverend Mother," the girls chanted. "No need to mention to our parents..."

"So, if you see our visitor in the corridor, remember your manners and say good morning."

A girl's hand shot up.

"Or good afternoon," Reverend Mother said. "Or good evening."

A faint sound of "Or good night" could be heard from an impertinent creature in the sixth form, but Reverend Mother let it pass and plonked herself down next to me at the table.

"Don't want any silly rumours to reach the parents," she said. "You know how much of a fuss they make if they think their daughters are in the middle of anything unpleasant."

"Quite so," Sister Barbara said, setting down her steaming plate of macaroni on the other side of me. "Pass the salt, please. I need something to make this palatable. Really, I have no idea why some of the parents don't just leave us alone to look after their daughters. They always want to push their noses in."

"Yes," Reverend Mother said. "It's staggering how much the parents feel they can interfere."

"As if they know anything about bringing up children! I ask you..." Sister Barbara picked up her fork. "Some of the ridiculous letters I've had from parents in the past...the stories I could tell...enough to make your hair curl..."

Rant over, she tucked in heartily, demolishing at least half of her plateful before turning to ask me,

"And how are you, dear Flora? I hope you've been relaxing."

"Oh, I'm fine," I said. "I've been sitting in the Staff Room all morning and now I'm ready for work."

Sister Barbara's eyebrows shot up. "You may be interested to know, Flora dear, that I always go for a walk in the woods around about 11.30 in the morning. I think I may have seen you – and heard you too – talking to a bird this morning. Perhaps?"

"Perhaps," I said, looking down at the stained table top.

From the pitying way Reverend Mother was looking at me, I felt confident Sister Barbara had already shared this information. Nothing was private at St Cecilia's. I chased the last piece of tepid cheesy stodge around my plate.

It just wasn't my day.

Coffee was served in the Staff Room.

"Thank heavens we're away from all that noise," one teacher said.

"Yes – positively ghastly, isn't it?"

"Such a shame we have to have lunch with the girls."

"At least we get to eat breakfast and supper away from the wretches."

I was all too familiar with the seemingly heartless way the teachers at St Cecilia's talked about their pupils – they didn't actually mean a word of it. Most of the staff at the convent were having the time of their lives and wouldn't have swopped their jobs for a million pounds.

"Are you sure you're ready to teach this afternoon?" Susie said to me. "If you're not up to it yet I can move things around a bit and cover your afternoon classes as well."

"No, I'm fine," I said. "Raring to go."

And I would welcome the distraction from my self-pitying thoughts.

"Tell you what," Susie said, "why don't you pop over to my house for supper tonight? I can take you home with me at the end of school and you can join us for a meal. I might make a quiche with gruyère cheese and mushrooms – I love mushrooms! Ages since we had a proper chat. I want to know all about the new violin teacher."

"That's kind of you," I said, "I love having meals at your house. You're a fabulous cook! But it's orchestra after school today and I really should be there to help Joe. It'll be the first time he's taken a rehearsal at St Cecilia's and you know what some of the girls are like."

Susie snorted. "I certainly do! Why I remember..."

"Someone mention orchestra?" Joe walked over to us. "Should I be worried?"

"Of course not!" I conjured up my brightest smile. "It will be fine! I'm looking forward to it."

We chatted for a while, then Joe drifted over to the other side of the room and Susie whispered in my ear, "There's sooner we have that chat the better; I can tell something's bothering you."

"You're right," I whispered back.

"OK then, supper tomorrow at ours," Susie said. "I insist!"

"Deal!" I felt better already. Susie was a wonderful friend to me, despite the age gap – discrete and loyal. I felt lucky to know her.

"Ladies," Reverend Mother said, coming into the room, "and gentleman," she added, indicating Joe, "might I disturb your post lunch coffee and introduce someone special? Sister Claire was so keen to join us that she's discharged herself from hospital and has this minute arrived by taxi."

"Hello everyone!" Sister Claire said. "Please excuse my appearance! I don't exactly look like a nun today..." She ran her hands over the shift dress she was wearing. "The nurses in the hospital very generously lent me some clothes as my habit has not yet been returned..."

"You look splendid," Reverend Mother said. "And that cardigan is such a pretty colour. Now, maybe someone would be kind enough to pass Sister Claire a coffee? Oh, thank you, Susie."

"I need to sit down," Sister Claire said. "I'm feeling..."

"Of course you do," Reverend Mother said. "The whole incident must have been quite traumatic. Over here – sit down next to Flora. I'm sure you remember her."

"I certainly do," Sister Claire said. "My saviour! And Mr Oak too."

"Please, call me Joe."

"Joe it is! Oh it's amazing to be here at last."

"Have you had lunch?" Reverend Mother asked.

"Well, yes, technically I have," Sister Claire said. "An NHS sandwich. They do their best but..."

Reverend Mother raised her hands in horror. "We can improve on that!" she cried.

"I could go to the kitchen and see if there's some macaroni left," Susie offered, already half way out of the door.

"Would you?" Reverend Mother asked. "That would be so kind."

Susie was always thinking of others.

"I would like to tell you, Reverend Mother, in confidence," Sister Claire said, "something about why I asked to come and stay here in the first place. It will help you understand about Grace and why she kidnapped me."

"In confidence, you say? Something about your story?"

"Yes; I can't reveal the whole truth yet, because I haven't spoken to someone who is an integral part of the story. It wouldn't be fair, without her blessing."

Sister Claire's voice dropped to a mere whisper and Reverend Mother craned her neck forward.

"Only if you're sure," Reverend Mother said. "You don't want to strain your memory. Things must still be a little fuzzy."

"Not at all," Sister Claire said. "Everything is crystal clear and I want to start getting things off my chest. Keeping a secret hasn't worked out too well so far, has it? Now, my story begins when I was born in England, not long after the end of the War."

"What part of the country do you come from?" Reverend Mother asked. "And why did you choose a convent abroad when you had been brought up in England?"

"Interesting questions," Sister Claire said. "I think I was inspired by visiting Rome. We went on a school trip to sing in the Sistine Chapel when I was a girl, and I fell in love with the place and the language. Joining a community there seemed the logical step. As for where I was brought up – Northamptonshire. A beautiful part of the world."

"I don't believe I've ever been there," Reverend Mother said, "but Sister Barbara went there once and I believe she liked it very much."

"I was brought up in Northamptonshire." Sister Claire lowered her voice. "But I was born in Dorset."

"Really? Which part?"

"Near Gillingham," Sister Claire said.

"What a coincidence! That you should be back here in Dorset now."

"No coincidence. This is the reason I've come back. I'm looking for someone from my past."

"Fascinating," Reverend Mother said. "Do let us know how we can help. So, you travelled all the way over from Rome to look for answers?"

"Yes," Sister Claire said. "The Reverend Mother

in my Italian convent said she was concerned to see me brooding and unhappy. She suggested it might be a good thing to investigate where I came from. It took a long time for me to acknowledge she was right – and part of me wishes I hadn't taken the plunge when I consider what's happened with Grace. Nevertheless, I think I have to see this through to the end. Investigating the truth can't be bad, can it?"

"That's a hard question," Reverend Mother said. "But I would say that in the end, truth will out. Perhaps it's better to search for it and face it head on – as long as no one is harmed."

"I'm glad to hear you say that," Sister Claire said. "Because, when I said I was born near Gillingham that was true, but I can narrow it down a little."

Reverend Mother creased her forehead.

"I was born here," Sister Claire said. "Here, at St Cecilia's. Please, Reverend Mother, tell me if I should reveal myself to my mother."

Reverend Mother plucked at the folds of her habit. "Goodness, yes, of course, I think you should, in fact I happen to know the person you have in mind will be thrilled to meet you again, however, you need to choose your time carefully. Let's adjourn to the Blue Parlour. Would you care to follow me, Sister Claire? I think it might be a more suitable place..."

The Blue Parlour was a serious room, used for important occasions like interviewing violin teachers and comforting the Head of Music when she's having a meltdown over her obnoxious ex-boyfriend and – well, I wasn't quite sure what this occasion was, but it was obviously of a delicate nature. I looked around the Staff Room. No one else seemed to have heard this intensely private conversation. I usually felt blessed as a musician to have good hearing, but on this occasion, I was beginning to feel embarrassed that I had over-heard so much.

Just then Susie returned, pushing the door open with her foot and carrying a tray.

"So sorry, Sister Claire," she said," but there was no macaroni left. I've made you a mushroom omelette. Is that all right?"

Susie's face was bright pink – must be from the heat of the frying pan.

"Oo, I love mushrooms!" Sister Claire said.

"We're on our way to the Blue Parlour," Reverend Mother said. "We need to have a chat. I'll take the omelette..."

Susie stood back to let the two nuns pass, her face now flushing scarlet, then she said loudly,

"May I come too? I'd like to – and you needn't be worried, either of you, because I know."

"You know?" Sister Claire said.

"You know." Reverend Mother nodded her head. "Of course – you would."

Susie took an enormous breath. "I know you're my daughter, Sister Claire, you're my own darling long lost daughter. I haven't seen you since the day I gave you up for adoption – the day I made the hardest decision of my life, to give you a chance with a proper family. Not a day has gone by for the last thirty one years that I haven't thought of you, wondered how you were doing and longed to hold you in my arms. I recognised you as soon as I saw you here in the Staff Room today. You're the image of my mother as a young woman."

Chapter 11

Sister Claire moved swiftly, flinging herself into Susie's arms with a cry of "Mummy!"

The tray flew high in the air, cutlery, plate and the omelette scattering widely, before landing with a clatter on the ground.

"My own little one," Susie murmured. "I thought this day would never come." She patted Sister Claire on the back rhythmically, soothing her sobs. "Thank you, thank you my darling, for wanting to find me, for having the courage to come here. It can't have been easy."

The two women clung to each other for ages, then pulled away. Two similar sets of soft brown eyes regarded each other – why had none of us noticed this before?

"There's so much to tell..." Sister Claire started.

"How long have you..?" Susie said.

"A while now, but I wanted to tread carefully..."

"So the adoption agency..."

"And I've already been in touch with my father, by letter..." Sister Claire said.

"And have you been happy? How was the family you went to? I have to know – have you had a happy life?" Susie wrung her hands together.

"Yes, they were wonderful – they are wonderful. You must meet them..."

Tears were pouring down Susie's face, Sister Claire's too – tears of anguish, tears of joy, tears of regret for what could have been – who could tell? All we, the observers, knew was that we simply shouldn't be there.

One by one, we melted away, until Reverend Mother was the last out of the room, closing the door gently on the two reunited souls within.

"Difficult thought it may be," she said to us as we stood hesitating in the corridor, "I think we should all go about our business this afternoon as if nothing has happened here today. We should teach our classes, look after the girls and generally do our duty. And not a word about this to anyone else, agreed? It is imperative that the girls do not get to hear the News. At least for now."

We all promised not to breathe a word and started to disperse.

"Wow!" Joe said as we set off for the Music Hut together. "And double wow!"

"There were clues," I said. "I'm sure you noticed, with your detective's hat on."

He wrinkled his nose. "I should never have told you of my boyhood dream about becoming a detective. But, yes, you mean about the mushrooms?"

"That's it – they both said they adored mushrooms."

"Mm, although it's fair to say that not everyone

who likes mushrooms is necessarily related. I quite like them myself."

"Fair point," I said. "But I'm sure I've heard them both say they like the colour green too..."

"I did notice that Susie was keen to get away as soon as she saw Sister Claire," Joe said. "She sort of gulped and then made that suggestion about wanting to go and get her some food. There was no need for her to do that – I think she wanted to get out of the room in a hurry."

"Oh, I thought she was merely being thoughtful," I said. "She's always offering to get people food. One of her main aims in life is to keep everyone properly fed."

"Yes, from what I've seen, she's very motherly."

Motherly – yes, a good description, especially under the present extraordinary circumstances.

"But she was pink in the face when she came back," I said. "I had thought that was because she'd got a bit flushed with the heat of the frying pan, but now with hindsight, I realise it's more likely because she was feeling flustered. More than flustered. On fire."

"Yes," Joe said. "A real case of out of the heat, into the frying pan."

We'd reached the Undercroft by now.

"What are all those scruffy bits of graffiti on the walls?" Joe asked. "I'm surprised the nuns haven't washed them off."

"Or even polished them?" I suggested.

"Ha ha!" Joe said. "But seriously, did the girls do

that? Doesn't fit in with the general order of the place. Weird."

"It's left over from the War," I said. "The nuns would never clean these walls; it would be like erasing the past. Sometimes they even bring classes of girls down to look at them as part of their history lessons."

"The War?"

"Yes; St Cecilia's was a rest home for American airmen. It was much too far for them to go back to the States for rest and recuperation when they had leave from their duties, and so they were sent here to relax and generally be waited on hand and foot."

"Did the nuns look after them?" Joe asked. "Somehow I can't see them doing that."

"Oh, no – it wasn't a convent in those days. The nuns didn't move in until 1945, after the end of the War. No, the building, Coombe House as it was called in those days, had been a grand country hotel and once the War broke out, it became a refuge for servicemen. It was very suitable, with masses of bedrooms and a large dining room already in place. I believe the Americans absolutely loved staying here – so grand, yet quaint and cosy."

"Amazing!" Joe said. He bent down to examine the wall more closely. "And so these graffiti...let's have a look. Ah, I see. There's a picture of an aeroplane here, signed *Bill*."

"Isn't it strange," I said. "I remember Reverend Mother pointing the graffiti out when I came for my interview and yet I've never really looked at them properly before. Oh, see here: *Russ loves Carol.* Sweet!"

"It's easy to forget how young these Americans must have been," Joe said. "I expect some of them were still in their teens."

"A very uncertain time," I said.

"Yes, I feel kind of sorry for them," Joe said, "so far from home. It must have been a comfort to find a local girl to love."

"Joe!" I said. "Come and see this. Do you think...?"

"What? Budge over a bit. I can't quite see. It's pretty dark down here..."

I pointed to the heart scratched into the plaster behind the door, next to a fire extinguisher. There were two names inside the roughly drawn shape, pierced by an arrow. *Hank* and *Susie*.

"Do I think it's our Susie?" I asked.

"I have no idea."

"Maybe she was here in the War," I said, "and met someone called Hank."

"How long has she worked here?" Joe asked.

"Oh, years and years," I said. "She once told me she remembered the first day the nuns arrived here, in 1945. She helped the cook prepare a vast meal to welcome them."

"So, perhaps she was already working here, in the rest home?" Joe suggested. "And stayed on when the nuns arrived?"

"Yes, possibly. She would have been very young," I said. "She's got a big birthday coming up next year – 50 – so in 1945 she would have been in her late teens."

"Old enough to work here," Joe said.

Old enough to fall in love.

"Ok," I said, "hear me out, bearing in mind this is pure speculation. What if Susie worked here towards the end of the War. She fell in love with someone called Hank, an American service man, and then because of everything being life or death, they got carried away, and then...well..."

"You mean, she became pregnant?" Joe said. "It has been known!"

I blushed. I didn't feel very comfortable discussing things like this with him. Not when he was quite so good looking and standing right next to me – and not when he obviously had no feelings for me whatsoever. And never would have.

"I do know such things happen," I said. "And we know something like this must have happened to Susie, or she wouldn't have had a baby to give up for adoption."

"She has another daughter at the school, doesn't she?" Joe said. "Diana?"

"That's right. Diana's a lovely girl," I said. "She's in the sixth form – and taking A level music this year, in fact I'm teaching her in about ten minutes."

"And Susie's married now?" Joe asked.

"Widowed," I said. "A couple of years ago. School choir sang at his funeral. Diana was in the middle of her O levels then. Terribly hard for her. And, naturally, for Susie. "

A sudden thought struck me.

"Goodness! I wonder if Diana knows she has a half-sister. In fact, I wonder how many people know about Susie's first child."

"Well, it seems Reverend Mother knew," Joe said.

I kicked the ground with the toe of my shoe. "Perhaps we shouldn't be talking about it."

"It's all right – there's no one around" Joe said.

He moved closer. Much closer.

"Flora, about what I said this morning, when you very charmingly appeared outside the window of my teaching room – that was a welcome surprise, by the way. Brightened my morning. I rather think you might have got the wrong end of the stick about what I said to you then."

"Really?" I looked up at him, at his smiling face, his twinkling eyes, and his soft lips which were threatening to move towards mine with the speed of a magnet leaping towards a piece of iron.

I took a step back. "Wait! Someone's coming. Can you hear footsteps?"

"I can hear voices too," Joe said. "And if I'm not very much mistaken, it's Susie and Sister Claire."

"Hello you two!" Susie said. She was arm in arm with Sister Claire, both of them wearing the sort of grins that would do a Cheshire cat proud.

"My mother," Sister Claire began, "my darling mother is going to show me something very special."

"Down here?" I asked.

So we'd been correct. Miss Marple, eat your heart out! Hercule Poirot too. There's a new pair of detectives in town.

"Yes," Susie said. "Immediately behind where you're standing."

Joe and I moved away, allowing Susie to inspect the tiny scratchings.

"Look!" she said. "Here it is! See?"

Sister Claire peered at the heart and read out, "Hank. Susie."

"Yes, Hank!" Susie said. "Hank – your father. Oh, we were so young."

Susie took Sister Claire's hands and clasped them to her bosom. "Whatever else you might be thinking, know this; you were a child born of love, a very deep love. I adored Hank."

Chapter 12

Now that Susie had shown Claire the graffiti in the Undercroft, her priority was to find her other daughter, Diana, and talk to her straight away. She didn't want any risk of Diana hearing about Sister Claire from another source. Even though Reverend Mother had asked everyone to be discrete, we all knew that it was only a matter of time before the news would be shared.

I hurried to the Hut, at Susie's request.

"Diana! Oh good, you're early for your lesson with me."

"Hello, Miss Gold," she said. "I'm very keen to show you the composition I've been working on. Shall I play it now?"

She sat down at the piano.

"Oh, I'd love to hear it – and I will hear it – but I'm terribly sorry, I won't be able to teach you today after all."

"Oh dear. Are you ill? I'm so sorry Miss Gold. You do look a bit tired."

"No, I'm fine," I said. "But thanks for your concern. It's just that, well, the thing is, er..."

Diana's eyes grew wide.

"It's nothing to worry about," I said quickly. "Your mother needs to have a word with you, a private matter – a family matter."

"Is she coming here?" Diana asked.

"No, you're to go to the Blue Parlour. Reverend Mother says you can stay there as long as you need to."

"The Blue Parlour? Sounds serious!" Diana said. "Are you're sure I'm not in trouble? The nuns aren't going to expel me or anything, are they? Let's hope they haven't found out I bunked off games last week – it was far too cold so I sneaked into the Hall and played the piano all afternoon."

Diana went off clutching her music case and sniggering as Joe sidled into the room.

"You OK?" he asked.

"Yes. You?"

"All very emotional, wasn't it?"

"Hello, Mr Oak," a small person holding a violin case said. "I've come for my lesson."

"I'll see you at orchestra," I said to Joe.

"Can't wait!"

I spent some time tidying up and getting a few things ready for tomorrow, but I couldn't settle. Looking out of the window, I could see a robin sitting on a branch.

"Wonder if you're the same one I shouted at earlier," I said. "Do you know what, I might have another walk and chat to you again."

As I strode down the path, I wondered how Susie and Diana were coping in the Blue Parlour. No doubt Reverend Mother had supplied them with plenty of tea and quantities of biscuits, the nuns' default answer to all woes.

I didn't want to speculate on what Susie might be saying to Diana, the same as I hadn't when she and Sister Claire had been left alone for the first time yesterday. All I knew was that a person as sensitive and thoughtful as Susie would be handling the situation perfectly. She must have wondered many times over the years if this situation would ever arise, and had probably already rehearsed comforting and generous things to say.

"Ah, there you are, Robin," I said as I spied the tiny creature. He began his chirruping song again.

"I'm sorry I was so rude this morning," I said. "You don't deserve to be shouted at, not a little bird like you." He fluttered his wings and took off over the woods. My heart followed, soaring up to the heavens.

What was it Joe had said? Shortly before he'd nearly kissed me? He thought I had perhaps got hold of the wrong end of the stick earlier. Did this mean that he cared for me? That when he'd said calling me his darling didn't mean anything, he'd meant to say it did mean something?

I walked on a little further, my shoes crunching on the piles of crisp leaves.

What would have happened if Susie and Sister Claire hadn't come down to the Undercroft at that point? Would Joe have kissed me? I closed my eyes and imagined what that would have been like.

"Hello dear," Sister Barbara said. "Out for a walk again?"

"Yes, hello!"

"So glad things are looking up for Susie," she said. "And Sister Claire. And dear Diana too. She will have a sister now – a great blessing."

I smiled.

"And, my dear," she added, "I do hope things will work out for you too."

I tilted my head back. "In what way? Do you mean with the concert? The choir?"

"With Mr Oak, of course," Sister Barbara said. "With your Joe. See you later, my dear. I might pop into orchestra to keep an eye on the girls."

As she carried on walking into the woods I thought I heard her murmur, "made for each other, those two."

Orchestra. I was looking forward to seeing Joe, for sure. I hoped the girls wouldn't be playing the sort of tricks that the last teacher had been subjected to. The time they had hidden their music up the fireplace chimney in the Hall had been particularly trying. Luckily I had managed to retrieve it before a fire had been lit, but some of the sheets still bore black sooty marks to this day.

"Ready?" I asked Joe as he stood at the conductor's stand in the Hall.

"As I'll ever be," he said, fiddling with his collar.

The stands were set out in front of him, music neatly arranged, all in place for the girls who even now were clamouring at the door. School lessons had ended for the day, they'd had tea and now were about to embark on orchestra rehearsal, an hour long endurance test – for the staff, that was.

I strode over and stood in front of the barbarians, hands on hips.

"There is to be absolutely no messing about today," I said, "I repeat, no silly behaviour of any kind."

Several girls looked disappointed and started grumbling – apparently I was trying to spoil their fun – while others were indignant,

"As if we'd do anything silly, Miss Gold," a girl said.

"Yes," agreed another. "We're the model of good behaviour."

"You're a model of something, but I'm not sure it's good behaviour," I said. "Come on, let's be having you. Take your places quickly and quietly, tune your instruments, then Mr Oak can begin."

I stood aside to let them flood in and as I did so, Susie appeared, beaming from ear to ear.

"Flora," she said, "I wondered if you'd mind awfully if Diana..."

"Of course I don't mind if Diana misses orchestra today, in fact I'd assumed she wouldn't be coming," I said. "You take her home."

I was desperate to ask how things had gone in the Blue Parlour, but felt unable to be quite that nosy.

"It all went fine," Susie said. "Diana's always

known she had a half-sister – it was never a secret within the family, but we all, that's myself, Bob and Diana, decided not to speak of it publicly."

So Susie's husband had known all along she'd had a baby before he married her – and that the baby had been adopted. How sensible too, to tell Diana all about it so that if the day ever came when the 'baby' contacted Susie, there wouldn't be a terrible shock or jealously to deal with. Just joy. I looked at Susie's beaming face. Pure and simple joy.

"Joe looks as if he's coping well," Susie said, glancing in at the girls sitting quietly in orchestra.

"Yes," I said. "Might be the calm before the storm, though. I'd better get back to him in a minute."

"Can't be too careful," Susie said. "Diana has been telling me about some of the things the girls used to do to the previous violin teacher – once they extracted the poor man's car keys from his jacket during the rehearsal, and he only realised when he tried to drive home."

"Amazing how they do these daft things when they're in a group that they'd never think of doing individually, isn't it?"

"Quite," Susie said. "And it was lucky on that occasion that Sister Barbara sorted it out so quickly. They all got a double detention that day, but Diana said it was worth it to see the look on the teacher's face."

"I'm keeping my fingers firmly crossed today," I said. "I've already warned the girls..."

"In case you miss me, I won't be in school tomorrow," Susie said. "Reverend Mother told me to take the day off – Diana too. Sister Claire's going to stay here at St Cecilia's tonight, then come over to us early tomorrow."

"How thoughtful of Reverend Mother," I said.

"Yes. I'm so grateful to her. She helped me out when I was lost, all those years ago. When the nuns first arrived here, I was working in the kitchen. It didn't take her long to spot my predicament – in fact she knew almost before I did that I was expecting. She was so unbelievably kind and didn't judge me, just helped and promised there would always be a job for me at the convent."

Susie lowered her eyes. There was a much longer story in there, and one which she might choose to share one day, but not here, not now.

"Anyway," Susie said, "the thing is, I asked you to supper tomorrow..."

"I'm not expecting to come round," I said. "Not after all that's happened. You have your day with Diana and Sister Claire."

"No, I insist," Susie said. "I want you to come."

"If you're sure?" I said.

"Absolutely. Oh, and bring your young man."

"My who?"

"Your young man – Joe, of course! Don't think I hadn't noticed that the pair of you were about to kiss when we came down to the Undercroft today. I'm sorry we interrupted you. Hope it won't be long before you two love birds get another chance.

I've got to go – Diana's waiting in the car. See you tomorrow. About six thirty?"

"Thank you!" I said.

I went back into the Hall, wondering why I hadn't heard much from the orchestra. The girls were being unnaturally quiet. There was a feeble attempt at music making going on – I could see the girls holding their instruments and swaying from side to side, but the amount of sound being produced was pitiful.

"Do they usually play this quietly?" Joe asked, waving his arms vigorously to try and raise the sound level.

"No, they most certainly do not," I said.

I clapped my hands. "Stop! Girls! Would you like to tell me what's going on? Why are you all so lacking in energy today?"

One girl put her hand up very slowly, letting her wrist dangle as if the fingers were too heavy for her to support them properly.

"Yes?" I said. "Would you care to enlighten me?"

"Well, it's like this," the girl said. "We are all feeling so, so ill – lovesick."

"Yes," another girl said. "We can't play properly while the pangs of unrequited passion sweep over us."

"We feel faint and are languishing with love for Mr Oak."

They all gazed at Joe, with their heads drooping to the side, rolling their eyes and generally looking completely ridiculous. He blinked rapidly and let his arms fall to his sides.

So that was their game! Pretending they had been overcome with love to the extent they could scarcely lift a bow or blow their clarinets and flutes.

"That is a shame," I said, "because if that is truly the case..."

"It is, Miss Gold, it is..."

"Yes, we simply haven't the energy..."

"If that is the case," I repeated, looking round the room, "I will have no option but to disband the orchestra immediately. We can do without you in the concert – after all, there are plenty of choir items."

A collective gasp of horror ran round the room as the girls considered their next move.

"And it will be a very great shame," I went on, "when I have to waste my time writing to all your parents to explain why the orchestra can't play in the concert."

Several girls frowned to hear this. I'd won a battle.

"And, of course, you will all be required to write a letter to Reverend Mother too, explaining why you felt you couldn't play your instruments in the usual way today."

Girls were conferring amongst themselves now, with lots of head shaking and shrugging of shoulders. Another battle victory.

The first girl put her hand up again.

"Yes?" I said.

"We all feel better," she announced.

"Hallelujah!" I said.

War over. Game, set and match to me.

I turned round to see that Sister Barbara had heard the whole exchange. As good as her word, she had slipped into orchestra to keep an eye on the girls' behaviour. She gave me a thumbs up sign accompanied by a megawatt smile that would have done Donny Osmond proud, and went on her way.

After that, the rehearsal went as well as it possibly could, with most of the pieces for the concert being tried though, and suggestions and comments from Joe being sensibly received by the players. They even offered to help fold up their music stands at the end of the rehearsal and take them down to the Hut.

Once we were alone in the Hall together, Joe wiped his sleeve over his face and gave a shudder.

"Not easy, is it?" he remarked.

"You did brilliantly," I said. "The girls won't be any further trouble."

Joe let out a long breath. "I'll take the conductor's stand down to the Hut, then I'll be off."

"I'll come with you," I said, picking up the folders of music.

We soon found ourselves down in the dark shadowy Undercroft again, on our way to the Hut. There was no one about. I don't know whether it was being in the same place as we had been before when we had nearly kissed, but something was making me tingle all over.

Joe put the stand down and turned to face me.

"I think we have unfinished business," he said hoarsely.

He was feeling it too.

I raised my face to his – and this time we weren't interrupted

Chapter 13

"I can't believe how much has changed since yesterday." I snuggled down in the passenger seat of Joe's Mini as we made our way to Susie's house for supper.

"Neither can I," he said. "Happy?"

"Oh yes!" The memory of Joe kissing me yesterday flooded into my mind for the billionth time. I wrapped the memory carefully in a soft blanket of joy and tucked it away in the deepest part of my heart.

"It's so kind of Susie to ask me along tonight," he said. "She hardly knows me."

"She's a very generous person," I said. "And thanks for giving me a lift. Hope it isn't too far out of your way."

"Hardly at all," Joe said. "And I'll drop you back at St Cecilia's afterwards, of course."

"Thanks," I said. "Complete lack of public transport in Dorset."

"I'd noticed! Particularly in the evenings. With the sort of work I do, I couldn't manage without my car."

"You must travel a lot."

"Yep. And did I mention I'm looking for a flat? Maybe a small cottage?"

"You did say something at your interview," I replied. "About staying with your parents for the time being but wanting to move into your own place eventually."

He sighed. "I've been looking around but prices are pretty steep. Have to build up my work a bit more before I can take on paying rent – let alone a mortgage."

"Carnegie Hall debut not on the horizon anytime soon then?" I asked.

"Sometimes I think I'd be lucky to be asked to play in the local village hall," Joe said, "although I do have a few concerts coming up in London, including one that's rather special. What I need is a big break – I need something astounding to happen, you know like that famous story about the singer."

"Don't think I know that."

"Apparently there was a student singer in the audience at the Albert Hall one evening when a soloist was suddenly taken ill. The conductor asked if anyone knew the part and would be willing to step in at short notice and the singer shot onto the stage, saying they were happy to give it a go. They sang the part superbly and the rest is history – their career has never looked back."

"Is that true?" I asked.

"Probably not, but it's a good story!"

We chattered on in an easy fashion for ages,

exchanging anecdotes from the world of professional music and getting more comfortable with each other.

Autumn trees were bending over the road, folding us in their dark spindly arms, releasing flurries of leaves as the wind pulled at their fingers.

"Nearly there, I think," Joe said as we rounded a corner and saw a row of cottages by a village green, dimly lit by a wobbly street light.

"Susie's house is the one on the end," I said. "You can park right outside."

"What a beautiful cottage," Joe said as I knocked on the door.

"Isn't it? I'd love to live somewhere like this."

"Maybe you will – one day."

Susie opened the door. "Welcome!"

"Are you absolutely sure we should be here?" I said, stepping into the hall. "We could have come round at another time."

"But I promised you supper tonight," Susie said.

"But surely you would have rather been on your own with, with..." Joe faltered.

"You can say it!" Susie beamed with happiness.

"OK. With your daughters," I finished.

Susie dropped her voice. "Actually, you're both doing me a huge favour. It's such an unusual situation, and having people here helps, in a funny sort of way. Makes everything seem more normal."

She showed us into the cosy sitting room where a welcoming fire was burning in the grate; her two daughters sat side by side on the sofa. There were over ten years between them and they'd never met before yesterday – but they looked as if they were already well on the way to becoming firm friends.

"Hello, Miss Gold," Diana said. "Mr Oak."

"Hello Diana," I said. "Hello, Sister Claire."

"Oh dear, this is tricky!" Susie said. "If no one minds, why don't we all use first names this evening? When you're back at school, Diana dear, you can call Mr Oak and Miss Gold by their full names, but for now, what about Joe and Flora? What does everyone think?"

Diana giggled. "I can't think of Miss Gold as anyone but Miss Gold. And I hardly know Mr Oak. So I'm going to stick to Miss Gold and Mr Oak, if it's all the same with you."

"Fair enough!" I said.

"I've been called far worse by pupils," Joe said.

"And what about me?" Sister Claire said. "Would you all like to call me Claire this evening? I'll be Sister Claire back at the convent but I would really love it if I could be Claire, here in my mother's house, with my sister."

She patted Diana's hand gently and threw Susie a tender look.

"Is that, er...is that your..." I faltered, thinking I was probably being a little too curious. As usual.

Susie said, "Yes! Claire is the name I gave her."

"I grew up as Claire," Sister Claire explained. "Susie named me before I was adopted and my adoptive parents saw no reason to change anything. In fact they always said Claire was the sort of name they would have chosen. They thought it suited me perfectly."

My shoulders relaxed. So I hadn't put my foot in it.

"And when I became a nun," Claire continued, "despite thinking about all sorts of other names, I decided to be Sister Claire to maintain that link with my birth mother – and also with my adoptive parents."

"How rude I am," Susie said, rushing over to the drinks tray at the side of the room, a tear glinting on her cheek. "I haven't offered you anything yet. Please, do sit down. Flora – what's your poison? Wine? Or we've got juice...what do you fancy?"

It was a good thing she had only asked me what I fancied, not who – because I was feeling a little distracted with Joe so close beside me.

Very soon we were gathered round the table while Susie ladled great quantities of food onto our plates.

"I know I said I was going to make a quiche," she said, "but in the end the weather was so chilly that I thought I'd make a warming beef stew."

"Looks magnificent!" Joe said.

"Plenty of mushrooms in it, though," Susie said, with a wink at Claire. "A family favourite."

"Indeed!" Claire said. "And Flora – when is this concert of yours? I hope I'll be allowed to sing in the choir."

"Oh, goodness," I said. "You'd be very welcome.

And I'm thrilled to hear you'll still be here then. I wasn't quite sure."

"My convent in Rome are allowing me to stay here for the rest of term," Claire said. "I'm thrilled too! I'll be winging my way back to Italy in time for Christmas." She turned to look at Diana and Susie. "But I do hope, now we've met at last, I'll be able to see you both regularly."

"That would be perfect," Susie said.

"Yay!" Diana said. "I've always wanted to visit Italy and now we have a relative living there."

"We have a guest room in the convent," Claire said, "and we're right in the middle of the city, so you'd be able to see all the sights. I adore seeing other countries myself. Being a nun these days isn't the same as in the past," she continued, perhaps noticing Joe's open mouth. "We're not locked up praying night and day. Well, some orders are, but not mine."

"I saw you were reading a book about America on the train," I said, "Are you planning a trip there?"

"Maybe one day," Claire said. She glanced at Susie, who gave a nod of her head. "I was trying to understand my heritage, too. I'll tell you something about my father."

"Hank?" Joe said

"Yes. It's about Grace, too."

"I'll stack the plates," Susie said. "Diana – would you mind giving me a hand? And I need to get the pudding sorted."

Susie and Diana slipped out of the room.

"They've heard all this before," Claire said, "but Susie said that it's fine if I tell you about it, particularly since you have both become somewhat involved in the mystery of Grace."

"You don't have to tell us anything," I said.

"No," Joe echoed, "especially not if it's private."

Claire clasped her hands together. "I want to. You both rescued me from harm in the hospital and I'm so grateful for that."

I sat back in my seat. At last the mystery would be explained.

"As I said before, I've always known I was adopted. My parents in Northamptonshire told me from the very beginning. I showed no particular interest in tracing my birth parents for many, many years, long after I had entered the convent in Rome. But then, I don't what it was, but a strange feeling grew within me. I wanted to know where my roots were, and what sort of people I came from."

"It must have been very hard," I said.

"It was." Claire sighed. "I had been worried about telling my adoptive parents how I felt, but they were brilliant and said they always thought this day would come. They encouraged me, and with the help of the adoption agency and my birth certificate, I took it from there."

"Pudding will be with you in a minute," Susie said as she put her head round the door. "Custard's nearly ready."

"To cut a very long story short," Claire said, "I ended up with the contact details of my father first, possibly because Susie was harder to trace, having married and changed her name, I don't know. Anyway, as soon as I knew where Hank lived in the States, I sent him a letter, explaining who I was and saying how much I'd like to hear from him. I told him I was going to be travelling to England to meet my mother, Susie, too."

"Wow," Joe said. "That took guts!"

"Yes," Claire said. "It wasn't an easy letter to write, particularly as I wasn't quite sure of the circumstances surrounding my birth." She picked up a spoon and began digging it into the tablecloth. "Soon he sent a friendly letter back, saying he hadn't known Susie had been pregnant when he'd been sent back to the States. He'd wanted to keep in contact with her, but it hadn't worked out that way for one reason and another."

"It must have been a tremendous shock for him," I said, "finding out about you after all these years."

"Yes," Claire said. "But he said over and over in the letter that it was a wonderful surprise."

"Does he..." I started, "is he..."

"No," Claire said. "No other children and no wife. He's recently split up with a long term partner and this is where it gets interesting."

She whipped a folded photograph out of the folds of her habit.

"See? He sent me this photo."

"He looks amazing," I said. "And who's that with him? She's looks a little like...no, surely not?"

Joe squinted at the picture. "Is it Grace?" he asked. "Hard to tell without the habit, but something around the eyes maybe?"

"Yes," Claire said. "Grace. Hank wrote in his letter that he was sorry the only photo he had was of him and his ex. Apparently she's a bit of a bunny boiler – his phrase, not mine. I'm not exactly sure what 'bunny boiler' means, but that's another story! Anyway, he said Grace still had a key to his house and was apparently in the habit of letting herself in and snooping through his letters when he was at work."

"Wow!" Joe said. "She sounds more than a little obsessed."

"Exactly!" Claire said. "I only realised that the lady who met me at the station last Sunday was his crazily jealous ex-girlfriend once it was too late. She must have travelled to England specifically to terrorise me – that's how unhinged she is. The rest of that particular episode you already know."

"But I still don't understand..." I said.

"Hank and I exchanged quite a few long letters," Claire said. "Hank knew I had arranged to come and stay at St Cecilia's at first merely as a visiting nun from Rome, not as Susie's daughter. I wanted to wait to reveal myself, to surprise Susie and tell her face to face who I was. I felt I owed her that."

"So Grace planned the whole thing after reading your letters?" Joe said.

"Yes," I said. "That explains how she knew so much."

"She knew when you'd be on the train," Joe said.

"And she hired a car and arranged to have somewhere she could take you to exchange clothes and tie you up," I said.

"No wonder she got in a state when she read in the paper that you'd been found and taken to the hospital..." Joe said.

"And I've remembered how she didn't want to join the choir – until Susie said she could sit next to her," I said. "She wanted to take a closer look at the person Hank hadn't been able to forget."

"Quite a tangled web," Claire said. "Grace sounds extremely resourceful – and you two sound like detectives!"

"Thank you!" Joe and I said together, then dissolved into fits of laughter.

"Good time for pudding?" Susie asked as she set a very welcome sight down on the table.

"Oh!" I said. "Crumble! Smells delicious."

"Here's the custard," Diana said, placing a steaming blue and white jug beside the dessert. "And some cream too, if you'd prefer it."

"What a feast!" Claire said. "Quite a treat after..."

She fell silent and blushed, then murmured, "I should have more charitable thoughts."

"Let me see," I said. "I know from personal experience that school supper was rissoles – again – last night. I'm guessing you didn't exactly enjoy them?"

Claire shook her head slightly, then her shoulders began to quiver and Joe joined in by sharing his experience of the baked beans with the unwelcome orange crust he'd been faced with on Sunday evening.

We were all helpless with mirth in the end, bonding round Susie's dining table.

"Let's have a toast!" Susie said, raising her glass.

"Yes, let's!" Claire lifted her tumbler of juice. "To the future!"

"To family!"

"And friends!"

Chapter 14

"Can we help with the washing up?" I asked Susie.

"Oh, no need for that." She looked across the table with pride. "I've got my two daughters to help."

"Yes, and I'm staying the night here too," Claire said. "Reverend Mother insisted. So I can help with breakfast before we all set off again in the morning."

"Splendid!" I said. "All sorted then. Well..." I glanced at Joe and he nodded. "I think we'd better be on our way. Thank you so much Susie, for everything."

"My pleasure! Now where did I put your coats?"

As we drove away, I thought what a very eventful time it had been since Sunday. Sister Claire had been kidnapped, rediscovered her mother and found a sister, and Grace had committed quite a few crimes, although the exact nature would be down to the police to decide.

And as for Joe, he'd rescued me from danger and captured my heart. Time would tell if anything would come of it.

I tried thinking about Charles for a moment and

found it wasn't as painful as usual, in fact there was scarcely any disturbance to report.

We sped on through the dark night, headlights picking out rabbits, and woods echoing with the strange cries of owls...

"Are you asleep?" Joe asked.

I sat up hastily. "Of course not!"

"Wouldn't blame you," he said. "Been quite a week so far."

"Exactly what I was thinking."

"I was wondering about Hank, over in the States," Joe said. "Wasn't it sad to hear that he never married and had a family?"

"Yes, it was."

"I'd like a family," Joe said. "One day."

We were about to turn into the school drive now.

"But not yet. I want to see life before I settle down," he added.

My heart plummeted. Couldn't you see life if you were part of a couple?

"What sort of things do you want to see?" I asked.

"Oh, everything! I'd like to travel. I don't always want to be teaching – my ambition is to tour the world, in an orchestra. It would be so glamorous, don't you think?"

"Maybe," I said. "Have you done much orchestral playing?"

"Oh yes," Joe said. "Loads of freelance work, all over – Switzerland, Germany, even Japan. That was a great trip."

"Sounds a lot of fun," I said.

More fun than being stuck in a school, obviously.

"Yes," Joe enthused. "I come alive when I'm playing on the stage. My ideal would be to travel for most of the year."

"Wouldn't you mind," I asked, "living out of a suitcase?"

"Oh no!" he said. "I love it! Total freedom to move on..."

"As long as the work is there," I said.

"Ah yes," Joe said. "It can be difficult to make a proper living as a concert violinist. But at least I've got some teaching now as well. That will keep me going."

Hmm. Did he mean until something better came along? Someone better?

"I remember you talked in your interview about your solo work," I said. "Anything coming up soon?"

"Big concert next week up in London," he said. "I'll miss choir on Tuesday, but I'll be in for orchestra on Wednesday. Have to alter my teaching timetable too, if that's OK?"

"Of course. As long as the girls all get their lessons at some point. And as long as the room timetable allows."

"And what about you?" Joe asked. "What would your dream job be?"

I thought for a minute. "Would it sound very boring if I said I'm already doing it?"

"Not at all! Each to his own, or, in this case, her own."

He pulled the hand-break and I started to open the car door.

"Allow me," he said and shot round to the other side. As I got out he leaned in as if to kiss me, then looked puzzled when I moved sideways.

"I don't want to alarm you," I said, "but if you turn round and look up, you'll see several nuns at the windows. I think maybe now's not the ideal time."

"Who cares?" Joe moved forward again, but I was too quick, turning so that he only pecked my cheek.

"Goodnight!" I said.

"Now, you're not intending to go down to the Music Hut, are you?" he joked. "I don't want to have to break down any doors, nothing like that because I haven't got my Superman costume with me this evening!"

I laughed and waved him off, noticing that a swarm of girls were peering out of dormitory windows too.

This was one of the many times I felt it might be better if I moved out into a flat in town to get a bit of privacy – however, the set up at the convent was very convenient and it suited me. I had learnt to accept the fact that nothing was secret at St Cecilia's. The girls were the nosiest crowd of people you could ever meet – surpassed only by the nuns, who seemed to live their lives entirely through others.

I began the long climb to Slum Alley and went to the kitchenette to make myself a coffee. As the kettle was boiling, I thought again about moving. If I lived in a little flat, I could have asked Joe in and made him a coffee, then listened to some music together and...I shook my head. No, not a good idea. I'd virtually only just met the man, for goodness sake!

And it was too soon after Charles. Maybe it always would be?

A soft knock at the door had me spinning round. "Sister Barbara!" I said. "Come in."

"I do hope I'm not intruding," she said.

"You're very welcome. Will you join me for a coffee?"

She put her head on one side, and coughed.

"Or maybe cocoa?" I suggested.

"Now you're talking!"

She settled down at the tiny table in the corner and waited patiently while I stirred some cocoa powder to a paste and boiled the milk.

"So," I said, handing her the comforting mug, "how can I help you?"

"Well, it's rather delicate," she said.

"Is it about Susie? And Sister Claire? We had a marvellous evening at Susie's – delicious meal – and they all seem to be getting on like a house on fire."

"Oh, I know all about that," Sister Barbara said. "I've already rung Susie and she's told me everything that went on. It's simply thrilling that it's all worked out so well. Reverend Mother is particularly pleased."

"Yes, Susie said Reverend Mother had been a tower of strength when she'd needed help," I said.

"Susie was so young," Sister Barbara said. "Younger than some of the girls here in the sixth form – probably about the same age as her own daughter, Diana..." She paused. "Reminds me a little of my sister's situation, although in many ways that was significantly different. My poor sister was taken in by a much older man who ought to have known better. And he was married." She sighed. "But that was a long, long time ago, back in 1910."

"Oh no!" I said. "So what happened?"

Sister Barbara rested her hands on her lap. "I did," she said. "I happened. My sister was only fourteen, and my mother looked after her throughout the pregnancy and birth and brought the baby – me – up as her own."

"So your mother was actually your grandmother, and your sister was your mother?"

"That's it," Sister Barbara said. "They didn't tell me until I left home to enter the convent. I believe this sort of thing happens more often than you'd think."

I cradled my coffee. "Well, Susie chose a different route."

"Yes, she did. And the adoption seems to have worked out fine for all concerned."

"Shame about Grace, though," I said. "Who would have thought jealousy could make you cross the world to try to take revenge? She didn't care who got caught in the crossfire."

"Like a Greek tragedy," Sister Barbara said. "But with a happy ending because Mr Oak came to your rescue and then you both saved Sister Claire in the hospital."

Why wasn't Sister Barbara calling Joe 'your Joe' anymore? 'Mr Oak' sounded very formal.

"Is there something you need to tell me?" I asked.

"You are very perceptive, my dear," she said. "I don't want to burst your bubble, but Reverend Mother has learnt something this evening – quite by chance, when she was chatting on the phone – that made us wonder..." Sister Barbara squirmed about on her chair. "I have to say, it might mean nothing, but after...after..."

"You mean after Charles dumped me last year and married one of my friends?"

"Yes. After that, I don't want to see you hurt again. None of us can bear it."

So, all the nuns had been discussing whatever it was – they all knew about it.

I crossed my legs. It would be nothing – maybe they suspected that Joe smoked a pipe, or had once had a speeding ticket. Perhaps he had left his teaching room in a mess? Whatever it was, it couldn't be that bad.

"How well do you think you know him?" Sister Barbara said.

"I only met him last Sunday, when he came for

his interview."

"So you've known him for four or five days?"

"Four days."

And five and a half hours. I studied my watch. Five hours, thirty three and a half minutes, to be precise. Not that I was counting.

"What's he done?" I said bluntly. "Tell me!"

"One of Reverend Mother's cousins works in the department store in town," Sister Barbara said.

"Yes?"

"And her friend, Mavis, works in the café there – you know, the one down in the basement?"

"I've been there – very nice cakes." I put my head on one side.

"They are, aren't they? With proper lace doilies, not those paper thingamabobs." Sister Barbara paused.

"And?"

"Mavis saw Joe, I mean Mr Oak, in the café with a lady."

I tapped my foot.

"He was leaning across the table," Sister Barbara said. "Holding her hand and whispering in her ear."

"What was he saying?"

Would Sister Barbara ever get to the point?

"Mavis wasn't near enough to hear, so she went over to ask if they wanted any more sugar. She heard Mr Oak say, 'You are simply amazing!' And then he kissed the lady's hand."

"But this could be nothing," I said. "And how did

Mavis know what Mr Oak looked like?"

"She'd seen him in a concert," Sister Barbara explained, "in the Town Hall. Apparently he was very good."

"It seems to me that Mavis is an interfering busybody," I said, "and I think she should keep her snout out!"

"Flora! You must be very tired."

"I am a little. Sorry!"

Sister Barbara put her hand over mine. "You see why I had to tell you," she said. "It might be absolutely nothing, but it was my duty to tell you."

"What did she look like, this lady?" I asked.

"Stunning, was how Mavis described her, with long blond hair, a turned-up nose and carrying a music case." Sister Barbara stood up. "Thank you for the cocoa, my dear. I felt I had to come and see you to impart this News."

'News' always started with a capital letter for the nuns.

"Especially as I do remember that I might have encouraged you a little to think of Mr Oak in a romantic way, before."

"You did," I said. "Most definitely."

"The general opinion now is that you should be careful. Goodnight, my dear! I will see you tomorrow."

I rinsed the mugs in the sink and then went to my room, feeling vastly deflated.

What if Sister Barbara was correct and Joe had been flirting recently with someone in the café? Or was involved with her in some way? I thought back to his conversation this evening in the car when he had said how much he valued glamour and excitement – he wanted to travel and explore, to live life to the full...he wanted to move out from his parents' house, maybe to have wild parties full of stylish and interesting people, dazzling musicians and talented artists...

I was boring and insignificant in comparison with this golden lifestyle. I felt a hard shell growing over me again – a hard protective shell, shielding me from hurt. This was the way forward: this was the way to survive.

I had forgotten to keep my distance – I wouldn't be making the same mistake again.

Chapter 15

When I woke the next morning, I felt more settled. Pottering about my room before breakfast I remembered how much I liked living in Slum Alley, with the friendly companionship of other staff in adjacent rooms and the late night chats in the kitchenette. The advantage of not having to commute to work was a bonus. Maybe one day I would move out, share a flat with friends, but for now I was content.

My job was very important to me – in a way, I was my job, I was married to my music. And the girls – they were like my children. Weren't they?

I heard some noisy shouts from the grounds outside.

"Oi! Get that coat on properly!" a voice yelled.

"It's too high! The pile of wood is going to fall over," another voice shrieked.

"Where's his hat? He can't be burnt without a hat."

It was November 5th – Bonfire Night, of course! The girls were dressing the guy and placing him on a towering stack of wood, ready to burn this evening.

The nuns always got very excited about Guy Fawkes, and seemed oblivious to the dangers of hordes of girls racing around massive flames. I was on duty tonight; as resident staff, we took it in turns to help supervise the girls at weekends. Not only was there Bonfire Night this Friday but on the Sunday there would the huge excitement of a film in the gym – promised by Reverend Mother to reward the girls if they promised not to tell their parents about all the business with the two Sister Claires.

"Hey, Flora!" a voice came from the next room. "You going down to breakfast?"

"Coming," I said.

"Me too!" a voice said from further down the corridor.

Very soon a gaggle of staff were walking down to breakfast, all very excited that it was the end of the week and all looking forward to Bonfire Night.

"Is that new violin teacher coming to the party?" one staff member asked.

"No idea," I said. "He doesn't work on Fridays, well, not here anyway."

"But I thought..."

"You thought what?" I tried to assume a blank look.

"Nothing. It's just that you seemed very friendly with him..."

I beamed brightly. "Goodness! It's part of my job to be friendly to all the music staff, isn't it?"

"Right...got it. Sorry! My mistake."

Wolfing down quantities of fried bread and sausages in the Staff Dining Room, I mentally ran over my day. Wendy the flute teacher was coming in this morning, and would be in the small teaching room. I'd have to help her move the music stands up to the Hall at lunchtime so that she could take Wind Band, then maybe persuade some girls to help me move them back...

"Hey, Flora," the history teacher said, from the end of the table. "Is it true what I heard about orchestra on Wednesday?"

"Mm what?" I said, my mouth still dealing with a particularly gristly sausage.

"I heard that all the girls pretended to fall in love with the new violin teacher – what's he called? Jamie? Jimmie?"

"Joe," I said, "his name's Joe."

Just saying his name made my heart race.

"Can't say I blame the girls," said another voice. "He is rather dishy!"

"Oo yes, those beautiful blond curls..."

"Bet he's a good kisser," an audacious voice said.

While everyone squealed with laughter, I toyed with the idea of standing up and screaming, "Yes, as a matter of fact he is, he's a very good kisser. The memory of his lips on mine makes me feel weak at the knees. But, do you know what, there's so much more to life than kissing and, and whatnot. If you must know, it's quite possible he's not reliable, because a friend of Reverend Mother's cousin, a woman called Mavis, well she saw Joe flirting in a café. I'm not sure who Joe was flirting with, but if he can do that sort of thing one minute then cuddle up to me the next, he's not the man for me. Not after all I've been through. And who cares anyway, because I'm a professional woman with no need of a man. I've got a career – teaching – it's important work. Ok, so it isn't glamorous like playing in an orchestra, touring the world, but I love it and I'm jolly well going to be the very best music teacher I can possibly be.

Of course, I said nothing of the sort but started mutely at my plate for ages, feeling a surge of boiling rage inside me, threatening to overwhelm rational thought and natural caution.

"Are you all right, Flora?" Sister Barbara's voice said at my elbow.

"Of course," I said. "Why do you ask?"

"Well, it's only that the Sisters here," and she indicated a stream of nuns with trolleys coming into the room, "they want to clear the tables. Your colleagues have long departed, and the bell's about to ring for Assembly."

Red-faced, I dashed out of the room, returning a moment later to pick up my hymn book from the side.

Sister Barbara clasped her hands high under her neck as if praying. "I do hope I didn't speak out of turn last night, Flora dear, and upset you in any way."

"Of course not," I said. "It's good to pass on information – can be very helpful when one is trying to make up ones' mind about someone."

I gulped, turned, and ran off towards the Hall, joining a throng of chattering girls surging along the dim corridor.

"Can't wait for tonight!"

"Yes! Reverend Mother says we can have sparklers!"

"Is the guy finished?"

"Not quite – got to find some trousers for him. He doesn't look right in just a hat, jacket and shirt..."

When I got down to the Hut after Assembly, Wendy the flute teacher was already there. She was the instrumental teacher I felt most at ease with and we'd become good friends since I'd started at the school a few years ago, in fact I considered her my best friend at St Cecilia's after Susie. I always looked forward to her smiling face on a Friday.

"Hi!" she said. "I gather I've missed the excitement of the week – the new violin teacher."

"Yes," I said. "He started on Tuesday."

"How was orchestra?"

"Fine! The girls tried a few tricks, but all sorted and Joe was fantastic at pacing the rehearsal. They got through most of the music for the concert at least once."

"Excellent!" Wendy flopped down on a bench. "And did you have a good half term? Haven't seen you since then."

"Oh yes," I said. "Had a lovely time with my

parents."

"No sightings of Charles?" Wendy asked.

Wendy was well aware of the fact that Charles and his new wife often stayed with his in-laws – in the village where my parents lived. Having helped me through my break up, she was knew how difficult this was for me.

"None," I said. "No sightings or even news of them, thank goodness. And how's it going with, er, what's-his-name? Hard to keep up..."

"You know full well what his name is," Wendy said. "But you can erase it from your memory bank because we split up over half term."

"You're not upset," I said.

It was a statement, not a question.

"You know I'm never upset! And I'm going out tomorrow night with someone new..."

"You're a terrible woman! Don't break this one's heart too, will you?"

The door opened.

"Joe!" I said. "I hadn't expected you to come in before next week."

"Don't mind me," he said. "I left some music here yesterday and as I was in the area I thought I'd pop in and retrieve it – got a chamber music rehearsal tonight with some friends and it's the only copy of the violin part."

"So, pretty essential," I said.

He nodded.

"This is Wendy," I said. "She's our flute teacher – takes Wind Band too."

"Hi!" Joe held out his hand. "Great to meet you."

Wendy's eyes grew luminous and she almost did a little dance, sweeping from side to side in the most astonishing way that I seriously began to fear for her sanity.

"Well, hello!" she said in a low breathy tone. "Welcome to St Cecilia's."

Joe shuffled back a step.

"Best be off," he said. "Busy day today. See you next week, Flora."

"You're not coming to the Bonfire Party tonight?" Wendy asked.

"Bonfire Party?"

She turned to me. "I'm surprised you haven't told Joe about it."

"I'd forgotten what the date was," I said, "until this morning, when I saw the girls messing about with the guy and gathering firewood."

"It's great," Wendy said, fluttering her eyelashes at Joe. "You should definitely come."

"Well," Joe said, "I've got my rehearsal..."

"Go on!" Wendy cried. "You know you want to!"

"I suppose I could pop in after the rehearsal." Joe glanced at me.

"Fireworks go off at seven pm," Wendy said. "Actually, it's usually only a few sparklers, but it's a lot of fun. See you there!"

After Joe had left, Wendy burst out with, "Why didn't you tell me?"

"Tell you what?"

"Why, only that Joe is the best looking man ever

to grace these hallowed walls! He's drop dead gorgeous! I wasn't going to come to the party tonight – it's usually terribly dull – but now I most definitely am. Bring it on!"

My heart sank. Should I say anything? What could I say? That Joe had kissed me and I'd thought something might have started between us, something magical and special, but since then I'd got cold feet, and was rapidly retreating to the safety of my shell again. What's more, I suspected that Joe wasn't quite the man I'd thought, in fact he might even be rather shallow with no intention of settling down any time soon, and possibly a massive flirt to boot. Mm, a bit like Wendy.

"Hi!" A small child carrying a flute case wandered in.

"There you are!" Wendy said. "Let's go next door for your lesson. Did you have a nice half term? How much practice did you do?"

"None at all. I was away with my parents in a caravan in Scotland for the whole week."

"Oh, sounds cold! Never mind, we can make up for it this week. Ten minutes a day at least – deal?"

The sound of raucous laughter told me that my pupils were on their way and I hastily got out the singing books.

Work – it was the only answer. If I threw myself into my teaching and concert preparation, then I wouldn't have to think about Joe at all. Or Wendy. And the way she had reacted to Joe.

Wendy and I went up to the Staff Room for a coffee at break time and sat in a huddle for a good gossip. As we always did on a Friday.

"I still can't believe how gorgeous that man is," she said dreamily, her head lolling back on the sofa.

"Who are you talking about?" asked a member of staff.

"Yes, that sounds like someone I want to meet," another said.

"Joe. Mr Joe Oak." Wendy said. "The new violin teacher."

"Oh yes, he's delicious!" a further voice said.

"He can tune my strings anytime!" a brazen member of staff said.

"Do we know if he's attached?" someone asked.

"Does it matter?" Wendy said. "He's fair game as far as I'm concerned."

I gasped.

"Only joking," she whispered to my shocked face. "Obviously if he was married or engaged, I would never..."

"I thought he was interested in you, Flora," the first member of staff said.

"Yes, that's what I'd heard," another said.

"Of course he isn't," I said. "Whatever gave you that idea?"

"Something Reverend Mother said."

"Yes, I thought Sister Barbara had mentioned it too."

"Pure rumour," I said. "Stuff and nonsense!"

"Well, that's a relief to hear," Wendy said. "First of all because I'm already half in love with him myself."

And second? What was her second reason? I couldn't stand this.

"I, I, er think we should go back to the Music Hut," I said feebly. "I think the bell must be going soon."

"And secondly," Wendy said, smoothing her skirt as she stood up, "secondly because I can tell that Mr Joe Oak is not the sort of man that Flora would ever fall in love with. He's simply not her type. No siree! Chalk and cheese. Not in tune with each other. It would never work."

I laughed heartily to hear this, shaking my head vigorously to show everyone how much I agreed that the very idea of Joe and myself would be too outlandish to be contemplated by anyone in their right mind.

Wendy was still cackling when we reached the Hut. Some best friend she was turning out to be.

Chapter 16

The flames roared as they took hold of Guy Fawkes, whooshing through him without mercy.

"Stand back!" I said the girls. "Don't get too close – it isn't safe."

"Have a hot dog, Flora dear," Reverend Mother said, passing me a greasy bundle wrapped in a paper napkin.

"Tomato sauce?" Sister Barbara asked, holding a plastic squeezy bottle over the sausage.

"And don't worry about the girls too much. Enjoy yourself! Have a good time."

"I feel I should watch out for them," I said. "After all, I am technically on duty here."

"The girls will be fine," Sister Barbara said, "while they're out here, anyway." She bit her lip. "I'm more worried about what they might do if they sneak inside. Remember last year?"

Sister Barbara was referring to the regrettable incident when several girls had stolen into the dormitories and upended all the beds.

"Ah yes," Reverend Mother said. "Yes. I do seem to recall some silly nonsense."

"They wouldn't do anything like that again,

though," Sister Barbara reassured her, "because they know that I wouldn't let them watch the film in the gym on Sunday if they misbehave."

"Hi! How's it all going? This is a tremendous occasion, isn't it?"

"Hello, Wendy," Reverend Mother said. "How nice of you to come this evening."

"Thought I ought to put in an appearance," Wendy said. "Show willing and so on."

It was the way she smirked when she said 'and so on' that bothered me. Quite a lot.

"Who else on the staff is here?" Wendy asked, looking around. "It's so dark, I can't quite see if..."

"All the resident staff are here," Reverend Mother said, "and lots of the others too. Some have brought their families – isn't that great? There's Susie over there, with Diana and Sister Claire. The police returned Sister Claire's habit today, so she looks more like her proper self. And there are quantities of small children too."

She pointed at a gaggle of little boys and girls buzzing around the food table having the time of their lives. "It's nearly time I got the sparklers out for the children."

"Good idea," Sister Barbara said. "I'll help you."

The two nuns wandered over to the food table. "Children! Time for sparklers. Gather round! Now, who'd like to write their name in the air with one of these?"

"Was there any member of staff you were looking for in particular?" I asked Wendy.

"You know there is! Joe. Is he here yet?"

"He didn't definitely say he'd come," I reminded her. "He said he had a rehearsal and he might come along later – that's all."

"OK, party pooper," Wendy said. "I know he might not come – but I thought it was worth turning up to have a crack at him."

"What about the man you're going out with tomorrow?" I demanded.

She shrugged her shoulders.

Then I heard a deep voice way above my shoulder. A low, smooth voice, the sound that I both wanted to hear most in the whole wide world and yet dreaded to hear. Joe's voice.

"Hi Flora!" he said. "And, er, Wendy, isn't it?"

"That's right! Fancy you remembering my name."

He stared at her, no doubt transfixed by her perfect bone structure, her beautiful eyes with their long lashes, her mesmerising charm...

I mentally slapped myself – why would I care what he thought of her?

"I need to go and talk to some of the girls over there," I said. "They're starting to throw bread rolls at each other."

"Seems par for the course," Joe said. "When I was their age I always enjoyed a good food fight."

"Me too!" Wendy simpered.

I rushed away, leaving them to their shared reminiscences of poor childhood behaviour. They were welcome to each other.

"Girls!" I said. "You shouldn't be chucking the food around."

"Sorry, Miss Gold," they said, "but it's such fun."

"Try and find something else that's fun to do," I said.

"We could go and stare at Mr Oak," one of the girls said.

"Mr Oak? He's not here, is he?" another said.

"Yes! Look, over there, talking to the flute teacher."

"Mr Oak! Oh, he's heavenly..."

"He's so good looking, isn't he?"

"Have you seen his Mini?"

"Yes – and do you remember when he parked it on the drive? Last Tuesday?"

"Yes, at three minutes past nine. I'll never forget that..."

"Nor me. When he stepped out of his car, I thought I would faint."

I stamped away. Had the whole world gone mad? Didn't they know what he was like?

"Everything OK, Flora dear?" Reverend Mother said.

"Fine!" I said. "Just fed up of the girls being idiots over Joe, er, Mr Oak."

Reverend Mother cleared her throat. "I believe Sister Barbara spoke to you yesterday," she said. "Passed on some News from Mavis? The friend of my cousin?"

"Yep, she did."

"I hope you didn't mind, but we thought you

should know."

"When did Mavis see Joe in the café?" I asked. Sister Barbara's News was forever seared into my mind, but I felt compelled to torture myself by asking to hear it all over again.

"I believe it was last week," Reverend Mother said, "shortly before he started at St Cecilia's."

"And was she sure...?" My voice trailed off miserably.

"She was sure he was very friendly with this woman," Reverend Mother said. "And before you ask, yes, Mavis definitely knew the man was Mr Oak because she'd seen both of them in a concert, playing together, violin and piano. Mavis thought the performance was superb, with a very special and unique chemistry between the two of them. When they bowed at the end, they held hands. And then kissed each other on the cheek – in front of the audience."

My head dropped down. So, not only did Joe have a close friendship with a lady, but she was also a musician. One good enough to play in concerts with him. A professional pianist – his accompanist. They must spend a lot of time working together, which is how they'd got so close, I supposed...

A mighty rage started building up in me. Before this latest revelation, I could almost have given Joe the benefit of the doubt, but now I was absolutely categorically sure he was a love rat. He'd had no business kissing me and making me feel as if he was the one. How dare he?

"I must go," Reverend Mother said. "I see some of the girls are leaping about a little too close to the flames – I believe one of them..."

I looked to where she was pointing and saw a girl being hit on the back by her friends. They were trying to put out the flames on her coat. Yes, that counted as a little too close in my book.

I grabbed a bottle of lemonade from the nearby table and ran over, but Joe was there before me, using his own jacket to beat the flames down.

"Lie down!" he ordered the girl. "Lie down, that's it. Soon have these flames out."

"Wow!" Wendy said. "That was spectacular, wasn't it Flora? Joe is a real hero."

"Mr Oak! Mr Oak!" the girls shouted. "He-ro! He-ro!"

"Well," Reverend Mother said, "saving another life – that's pretty stupendous."

Some of the girls started laughing hysterically then crying with the drama of it all and Sister Barbara decided enough was enough.

"Inside, all you girls," she said. "Party's over. What you were doing cavorting so near the flames is beyond my comprehension. Now, remember..."

"Yes, Sister Barbara," the girls chanted, "we know. Don't tell your parents in your next letter home."

"There's absolutely no need," Reverend Mother said, "because nothing bad happened, did it girls?"

"No, Reverend Mother."

"And don't forget, there's a film to see in the gym on Sunday," Sister Barbara said, "so the celebrations of the weekend aren't over yet."

The girls melted away and I wandered about with the other staff collecting food debris and generally tidying up. Joe quenched the bonfire flames by pouring a bucket of water over them.

"What next?" Wendy said. "Pub?"

"Great idea," Joe said. "I can give you a lift in my Mini if you like."

"No, you're OK. I've got my car," Wendy said, "but maybe another time?"

"Sure," Joe said. "Flora? Will you be joining us?"

"Can't," I said. "I'm still on duty, more's the pity. The girls will be as high as kites and won't want to get ready for bed after all this excitement."

"What time do you finish?" Joe asked.

"About half an hour."

I turned to trudge my sad way to the dormitories, but Joe rested his hand lightly on my shoulder, saying, "Come round to the front when you've finished – I'll give you a lift."

"You don't need to," I said.

"Come on, Flora!" Wendy said. "There'll be a whole crowd of us in the pub in town, you know there will. It's always lively on a Friday night. Please come."

"Pretty please?" Joe asked, his eyes shining brightly in the moonlight and the smell of the fire still lingering on his singed jacket.

"Ok," I said. "Give me half an hour."

The girls were as impossible as I had anticipated and it was more like three quarters of an hour when I finally reached the drive where Joe was sitting alone in his Mini.

Oh dear. I had thought he might be giving a lift to some other staff too. Not sure I would have agreed so readily if I'd realised it would only be the two of us,

I sat as far away as possible from Joe as we drove along.

"Is there anything wrong?" he said eventually, breaking the strained silence.

"Wrong?" I said. "Whatever gave you that idea?"

"I feel as if I've offended you in some way."

"No. Can't think of anything."

"Your friend Wendy's a lot of fun," he said.

"Yes, isn't she?"

"Says she wants to come to my concert next week in London."

"Really?" I squeezed my fingers tightly.

"Flora," Joe began, "I don't suppose there's any chance that you might be able to come and hear me? I know it's a long way..."

I gave an incredulous laugh. "You think I can spare the time to trek all the way up to London midweek and go to a concert? With my duties here and the concert coming up?"

"No, of course not," he said. "Forget I mentioned it. But I'd love you to come and hear me play one day. It would mean a lot to me."

I didn't speak again until we reached the pub –

my throat felt too tight.

"Hi!" Wendy shouted over the hubbub when we arrived. "I've got the drinks in. Joe – you're sitting next to me."

Joe looked at me, then did as he was told. I walked all the way round the table to sit with some of the other staff, plastering a jovial smile on my face. I tried to follow a conversation about the best way to teach geography to the Upper 4, all the time listening to snippets of what Wendy and Joe were saying.

"So, you'll leave a ticket for me at the Box Office in Wigmore Street?" Wendy said.

"Yes..." Joe said.

"How much do I owe you?" Wendy started fumbling in her bag.

"Nothing," Joe said. "Please – I mean it."

"That's so kind...and well done you, for playing at the Wigmore Hall."

"Yes," Joe said. "It's the first time I've played there..."

"Your debut! Oh, fingers crossed," Wendy said. "I'm sure it will go swimmingly. We must go for a drink afterwards...wait, I don't think I can stay so late in London, because I'll miss the last train back down here..."

"Don't worry," Joe said. "I'll give you a lift back. I always take the car when I'm playing up in town. I know the parking's a nightmare, but it's great to have the total freedom of being able to drive back whenever you want even if it's the middle of the night..."

"Oh, I do so agree..."

I put my hand to my throat, feeling quite nauseated. When one of the geography teachers said she was driving back to St Cecilia's because she had an early start due to a field trip the next day, I begged a lift, made my excuses and left.

Once back in my room I remembered another terrible Bonfire Night when I'd had chicken pox as a child. My parents had arranged a party in our back garden. I had been allowed to stand on my bed and look out at my family and friends running about, setting up the fireworks and scoffing delicious food. I could see everyone enjoying themselves while I was trapped behind a sheet of glass. However much I beat on the window, I wasn't allowed outside to join in.

I still felt like that sometimes.

Chapter 17

"Morning, Sister Claire!"

"Hello my dear," Sister Claire said as we passed in the corridor. "Wasn't the Bonfire Party on Friday fun? I really enjoyed it. I stayed the rest of the weekend with Susie and we had a marvellous time."

"Glad it's all going so well," I said. "And yes, the party on Friday was quite an occasion. Still, back to the grindstone now – another week, lessons to teach."

"And for me too," she confided. "Sister Barbara has suggested that I might like to teach a few Italian lessons while I'm here and I'm only too glad to oblige. I will feel I'm imposing less if I can do something useful during my stay at the convent."

"What a great idea," I said. "You must be very pleased. Watch out for the girls though. They aren't always that well behaved."

"I was a convent girl myself," she said, "and I work in a convent school in Rome. I know exactly how to treat the girls."

"I don't doubt it!"

"And I'm starting to teach Susie some Italian

too," Sister Claire said. "I'm hoping that she and Diana will come out and visit me once I'm back in Rome."

"How lovely!" I said. "It's all working out so beautifully."

"And how are you getting on," Sister Claire asked, "with your young man?"

"He's not my young man," I said, "he's a colleague."

"But I was so sure," she said, "when we all had supper last week...the way he looked at you. Not that I know much about affairs of the heart, being a nun, but nevertheless I'm surprised."

I smiled through clenched teeth. "Must get on," I said. "My class will be waiting for me by now."

Keeping busy was the only way I was going to cope. When I reached the Hut, I was pleased to see an enormous pile of papers on top of my piano. Good – so the girls had taken me at my word when I'd said they should try to finish their compositions for our annual Christmas Carol Competition over the weekend. I would enjoy ploughing through those.

At break time, I dismissed my class and sat down at the piano to try a few of the girls' carols. I wouldn't be going to the Staff Room for coffee – I had far too much to be getting on with to waste my time socialising. And I couldn't face anyone.

I picked up the first piece. Scanning through the words, I noticed with amusement that there was a robin in this version of the Christmas story, perched on top of the stable in Bethlehem.

Robin redbreast sweet and clear
Appearing now to dispel fear;
Song so light and special here
Joy to bring to mortals mere.

Ok, so it wasn't going to win any prizes for poetry. Maybe the tune would be better?

I stretched my hands out and improvised some chords while I sang the words to the tune the girl had written down.

"*Robin redbreast sweet and...*"

"Wow! That sounds good," Susie said. "Who wrote that one?"

"Hiya" I said. "Thought you'd be having a break time coffee upstairs now."

"I thought you would too," Susie said. "When I saw you weren't, I decided to come down and find you."

"If you're really interested," I said, "this particular masterpiece – *Robin in the Stable* – is by the girl who stood too near the flames on Friday at the Bonfire Party. So near that she caught fire!"

"Yes," Susie said. "We saw that. It was quite frightening. So glad no one was hurt. Joe was a hero yet again, wasn't he, helping to put the flames out by throwing his jacket over her?"

I looked down at my lap. I'd known Susie would bring the conversation round to Joe. An enormous fat tear ran down my face, splashing onto the back of my hand.

Susie was at my side in an instant. "What is it, sweetheart?" she whispered. "I can't bear to see you so unhappy. I thought something was wrong on Friday evening but didn't get a chance to talk to you with all the girls around."

"You don't want to know," I said. "You've got enough on your plate with your new family member."

"If it hadn't been for you and Joe," Susie said, "I don't think I would have met Claire. You saved her life! I owe you both so much. Tell me – what's gone wrong? When you and Joe came for supper last week, you seemed to be perfectly in harmony with each other. How can things have changed in so short a space of time?"

"I don't think Joe's the man for me after all."

Susie held me in her arms and I told her all about the hard shell that had grown back over me and about the way I still got upset when I thought about Charles' betrayal. I told her how Joe had kissed me after Orchestra and how I felt as if I'd died and gone to heaven, but then when Sister Barbara had told me what Mavis had seen, I had begun to doubt him. Reverend Mother had added to that mistrust by revealing fresh details at the Bonfire Party.

"And even before then," I said, "when Joe gave me a lift home from supper at your house I began to feel uneasy. It all seemed so fast. I'd only known him a few days and I was pinning all my hopes on him. It was totally unrealistic. In the car on the way home he started talking about how his ambition is to travel and play full-time in an orchestra. He wouldn't be interested in someone like me, not a mere school teacher. He's way out of my league."

Susie took a tissue out of her pocket and gently wiped my eyes. "Nothing you've said so far is conclusive proof of anything."

"But I haven't told you about going to the pub with him yet," I said, "after the Bonfire Party."

I cried a bit more and told her about the other Bonfire Party when I was seven and the feeling of being trapped behind a sheet of glass with everything exciting happening outside.

"I feel as if I'm an observer," I said, "waiting."

"It takes a long time to get over a disappointment," Susie said. "I think you're still coming to terms with the whole Charles situation and how he treated you. Not all men are like that – I promise you they aren't. And good things do happen, even if you have to wait an awfully long time. Look at me!"

"I'm so selfish," I said, blowing my nose. "How are you getting on with Claire?"

"It's early days, of course," Susie said, "but so far I can honestly say that Claire being part of my family is an overwhelming joy. I'm not going to kid myself –I know there might be tough times ahead and there's the whole issue of Hank to face."

"I wondered about that," I said. "What's the next move?"

"Well, the plan at the moment is that we're

going to telephone him in the States this week and have a good chat. And who knows, if all goes well, he might even come to visit while Claire is still here in England."

"Wow!" I said. "That's huge! How do you feel?"

"Not sure," Susie said. "Bit scared, but I'm optimistic."

She put her arm on my shoulder. "And that's what I want to say to you, Flora. Be optimistic, look to the future – because things have a funny way of working out, you wait and see."

"Not in this case," I said. "And I can't believe that Joe asked me to go to his debut performance at the Wigmore Hall this week and I was mean enough to say no."

"Is that a big thing then, for a musician," Susie asked, "the Wigmore Hall?"

"Yes," I said, "it's a highly prestigious venue, and of course you only make your debut once. It's massive for a musician. He will have worked for years to get that date, and I turned down the opportunity to go and hear him." I sniffed. "And so Wendy is going."

"Wendy won't really be interested in him," Susie said. "You know what she's like – she eats men for breakfast! Wolfs them down and spits them out, then it's on to the next one."

I grinned. "Pretty good description, though not entirely flattering for Wendy."

"Sometimes it's hard to believe what good friends you are," Susie said, "but you are, aren't you?"

"Yes," I said. "You and Wendy are my best friends."

"So, you don't have to be similar to someone to get on, do you?"

"Of course not," I said.

Susie put her head on one side.

"Ah! I see what you mean," I said. "Just because Joe has different ambitions to me and is probably more extrovert, doesn't mean..."

"That you're not soulmates," Susie finished for me.

"But there is the small question of what Mavis saw in the café," I said.

"A friend of a cousin of Reverend Mother? You're taking her word as gospel?"

"It does sound a bit stupid, doesn't it?" I said. "But then there's Wendy, and Joe's concert..."

"You should go to that concert," Susie said.

"I can't spare the time. Besides, someone would have to cover my lessons. And there's choir to consider."

Susie tapped the side of her nose. "Leave it with me! I know someone who has recently joined the staff, in fact I happen to be related to them."

"You mean Sister Claire?"

As Susie nodded, the bell went and a low rumbling could be heard – the approach of thundering feet belonging to girls who I felt sure were anxious to hand over yet more carols for me to consider.

"I will see you at lunch time," Susie said, "in the

Refectory."

"I haven't got time for lunch! I've got so much work – planning to have a sandwich down here."

"I thought you'd say that. So when I tell you I will see you at lunch time in Refectory, I jolly well mean it, OK?"

"OK!"

I knew when I was beaten.

I went up to the Refectory at midday and attempted to eat a strange chicken pie that was mostly pastry and white sauce with two chunks of chicken, three peas and a slice of carrot hidden inside – plus the obligatory baked beans as an accompaniment. Despite her promise, Susie wasn't there, but I chatted to my colleagues and felt more normal.

Susie had been right; hiding away in the Music Department wouldn't have done me any good at all. Whatever was going on with Joe, memories of Charles, my ever growing shell, Wendy, the Wigmore Hall recital, all of it – I still had to keep marching on and make the best of my life.

"I'm so sorry," Susie said, rushing in as the coffee trolley appeared in the Staff Room. "So glad I've found you in here. I really had hoped to have lunch with you, but I was delayed. Few things to sort out."

"What's going on?" I asked, passing Susie a large coffee.

"Thanks." She sat down beside me. "I hope

you'll be pleased with what I've arranged. You're not teaching tomorrow afternoon. Sister Barbara is taking one of your lessons and Sister Claire the other. You'll leaving straight after lunch – I'm driving you up to London to go to Joe's concert."

"But what about choir?"

"No worries," Susie said. "It's moved to Thursday – just for this week."

"I haven't got a ticket for the Wigmore Hall."

"Reverend Mother has been on the phone and bought two tickets, one for each of us; they'll be waiting at the box office."

I opened my mouth and took a deep breath.

"And if you're trying to think of objections," Susie said, "don't bother – it's all fixed and that's final. I'll be driving you home as well, so you needn't worry about that. I know you'll have a rather late night but Reverend Mother said there's no need for you to play in Assembly the next morning, and if you want your first lesson covered as well, it won't be a problem. Sister Claire's very keen to help."

"I don't know what to say! Except that you've been very busy and I'm incredibly grateful. Sorry you missed your lunch."

"Do me good to skip a meal for once!" Susie said. "And there's more to tell, if you want to hear some good news."

"Bring it on!"

"OK," Susie said. "Reverend Mother was speaking to her cousin last night, the one who is a friend of Mavis, and the cousin happened to mention that Mavis was prone to exaggerate and had a rather over-active imagination. For example, apparently once Mavis had reported to the manager that there were definitely rats in the café kitchen because she'd heard some strange noises – turned out it was merely some builders next door she could hear through the walls..."

I sat up very late that night in the Hut, trying to sift through as many carol compositions as I could, so that I wouldn't fall behind with my work by making the trip to London.

One of the girls' compositions made me smile.

The Christmas star shines for us all
The dawn of new hope is nearly here;
The whisper of love is alive on the earth,
The bells ring out loud and clear.

"Yes," I said. "I admit that at least the suggestion of hope and love might be on the horizon. We shall see."

Chapter 18

"I don't know what to wear," I whimpered.

Clothes lay discarded all over my room in Slum Alley. There was a red silk blouse hanging on the mirror, a pair of black trousers draped over the dressing table, a couple of Laura Ashley dresses on the bed and a jumble of separates littering the floor.

I had chosen an outfit earlier that morning before teaching, but now it was time to get dressed ready to go to London, I'd lost all confidence.

Looking out of the window I could see Susie walking to her car. Heavens! I was that late! My hands shook as I picked up handfuls of clothes and stuffed them into the bottom of the wardrobe. What did it matter what I wore? This was Joe's debut concert – it wasn't about me.

I threw on the outfit I had originally selected, the red blouse and trousers, added a long glittery necklace, grabbed my bag and coat and fled downstairs.

We made good progress on the road to London, arriving with plenty of time to spare and managing to find an incredibly convenient space near the Wigmore Hall. My bag felt heavy with so much loose change – I knew from previous experience how much the meters would demand for the privilege of parking on the street.

"It's so exciting!" Susie said. "I haven't been up to town for ages."

"Me neither!"

Then, on the other side of the road, I saw Joe coming down the steps of the Hall. He looked just about as wretched as all musicians do before they give a big concert, as if they'd rather be anywhere else in the world and a member of any other profession. My heart went out to him.

"Let's go and say hello," Susie said.

"Best not," I replied. "He hasn't seen us."

"You're wrong," Susie said. "He's definitely spotted us, well, you at least. He's coming over."

Joe looked to left and right as he checked the traffic, giving me a chance to admire his fine profiles. Flawless – from both sides. And then he was in front of me.

I stood on one leg, my foot ridiculously twisted round the other ankle, and grinned inanely.

"Flora! I didn't expect to see you," he said. "After we spoke about my concert in the car I remembered that you would never have been able to come because it clashed with choir."

"There's more to life than music rehearsals," Susie murmured.

"Choir's moved to Thursday," I explained. "Only for this week – courtesy of Reverend Mother. Is

Wendy coming to your concert? I haven't seen her."

"No, I've not seen her either yet, but it's still very early. She said she'd like to come and I've left a ticket at the box office for her." Joe put his hands in his pockets. "Your friend Wendy's quite a character, isn't she?"

"Oh, yes," I said, "she certainly is!"

Joe frowned. "Where did you get to after the Bonfire Party? One minute you were there in the pub, then the next you'd vanished."

"I felt a bit tired," I said. "Got a lift home with the geography teacher – didn't feel quite myself."

"Well, as long as it was nothing I said."

"This is no good, chatting in the road," I said. "You're about to do a major recital! I'm sure you should go off and practise, have a snack or something."

"I couldn't eat a thing," Joe confessed. "I'm going to walk around the block a few times.

Calm myself down."

"You do that," I said. "Good luck! Break a leg and all that – see you on the other side."

"Yes, come and find me in the foyer afterwards," Joe said. "You too, Susie! I'd love to know what you both thought of the programme. Oh, look!" Joe pointed across the road. "Isn't that the critic, you know, the well-known one?"

I squinted down the street. "I think you could be right."

"Is he very famous?" Susie asked.

"Yes," Joe said, "but for all the wrong reasons. He has the reputation of being one of the meanest men in London – particularly harsh in his criticism of young string players making their debuts."

"You'll be fine," I said. "It's going to be great, and yes, we'd love to come and meet you afterwards, wouldn't we, Susie?"

"Try and stop us!" she said.

Once inside the extraordinary pink and gold hall, sitting near the front, I found myself clenching and unclenching my fingers, feeling terrified for Joe. The hall was nearly completely full. I turned round to see if I could see Wendy, without success.

"Perhaps we'll find her in the interval?" I whispered to Susie.

When Joe first walked onto the stage, there was a terrific burst of applause. As soon as he started playing, I instantly relaxed, swept away in a glorious swirl of notes – transported to another world.

"He's ever so good! I'm no musician, but I can tell he's really talented," Susie said in the interval as we clutched our drinks in the large crowd gathered in the foyer.

"Let's make our way over there," I said. "Towards the critic. I'd be interested to hear his verdict."

"OK," Susie said. "Excuse me...do you mind? May we just get through...thank you so much."

Eventually we managed to position ourselves behind the famous but harsh critic.

"Not bad, for a debut," he was saying, "not bad

at all, although this young man will have to watch out in the second half because he has chosen a very ambitious programme for a musician of his age. I remember hearing the last piece in Vienna a year ago – that performance would be hard to surpass, but I'll reserve final judgement until..."

Susie grinned at me.

I gave a little jump. "Yes! Looks as if it's going to be all right."

"Hello, you two. Fancy seeing you here!"

"Hi, Wendy," I said. "Wow! You look fantastic."

"So do you," she said.

I felt myself fading as I remembered Joe had offered her a lift home.

Wendy drained her wine glass and popped it on the side. "Well, that's me done," she said. "I'm off out to dinner now."

"You're not staying for the second half?" I said.

"Oh no," she said. "You need to keep up, Flora! I promised Joe I'd come and hear him and I have – well, some of the music anyway. I was a teensy bit late."

I felt my eyes widening until they almost filled my whole face.

"Anyway," Wendy continued, "do you remember I said I was going out for a drink with someone on Saturday?"

"Yes..."

"To my surprise, he turned out to be rather nice, so I'm focussing on him now." Wendy glanced at her wrist watch. "He should be waiting for me outside right now. We're going out for drinks, then dinner and who knows, maybe a nightclub too. I'm so excited!"

I felt torn between feeling a little bit disapproving – and wanting to throw my hands into the air and scream, "Hallelujah!"

"Flora?" Wendy said. "Everything all right?"

"I'm fine," I said.

"Have a lovely time," Susie said to Wendy.

"I intend to! Tell you what, if you do happen to see Joe after the concert, would you give him my apologies and say I couldn't stay for the second half. And obviously, I don't need a lift home."

"We'll tell him," I said, "if we see him."

The bell rang for the second half and we took our places eagerly.

"Well!" Susie said. "Bold behaviour, even for Wendy."

As Joe and his accompanist walked on stage, I realised I hadn't even looked at the musician playing the piano. It definitely wasn't the person that Mavis had spotted in the café, because this pianist was well into middle age and his hair was grey.

If it were possible, the second half was even better than the first and I felt sure that the critic would be able to give his approval. The audience went wild at the end, with most of us jumping to our feet.

"Encore!"

"Bravo!"

"Never heard anything like it!"

Joe played two encores, the first a sad and sweet minuet that brought a tear to the eye of everyone there. The mood changed with *The Flight of the Bumblebee*, his fingers moving furiously to complete the sparkling virtuosic runs faster than had ever been heard before.

"I feel so proud," I whispered to Susie.

We waited outside in the foyer with a crowd of fans for ages then finally the shout went up.

"He's on his way!"

"Here he comes!"

"Three cheers!"

I looked around at the people from all the different areas of his life waiting to congratulate him. Some of them were probably family, others must be college friends and former colleagues.

Susie whispered in my ear, "You're probably going to get to know quite a few of these people before too long."

I smiled and with the back of my hand batted away her absurd ideas. For now, I just wanted to see Joe and congratulate him. The concert had been sublime.

Then I saw him standing there, handsome, elated, all the tension gone. He seemed to look straight at me.

"Joe!" cried a voice from directly behind me. "How superb you were tonight, darling! I'm so proud of you – you were phenomenal!"

Within seconds, a tall glamorous blonde with an upturned nose had thrown herself into his arms and kissed him on both cheeks. He put his arms around her in an enormous bear hug. His other accompanist! The one Mavis had seen in the café. His girlfriend.

"Let's go," I said to Susie. "Please, quick, I can't do this. I don't want to see him. I've changed my mind about seeing him – I mean I have seen him but I don't need to speak to him."

"I'd like to say hello and to thank him," Susie said. "Apart from anything else, I need to pass on the message from Wendy – that she was here for the first half and doesn't need a lift back."

"You can if you want to," I said. "I'm going to go and wait by the car."

I fled from the hall before I fell apart. How could I have got it so wrong?

Standing by the car, I looked up to the sky.

"Back there," I said to the faint city stars, "back there in the hall is a young man I love – and he's in the arms of another."

Could life be any more cruel?

Chapter 19

I was up bright and early the next morning, well, early anyway. I'm not sure that bright was a word that could have been applied to me, to be honest.

The journey back to Dorset in Susie's car had been very quiet. I'd pretended to be asleep most of the time so that she wouldn't ask me anything. When she dropped me off at the convent, she said,

"Joe asked if you had enjoyed the concert; he was surprised you hadn't waited to talk to him afterwards in the foyer."

I hadn't trusted myself to reply, but fled into the building sobbing, not caring if I woke any pupils or nuns.

It was only when I got up to my room that I realised I hadn't thanked Susie for her very great kindness in organising the trip, and especially for driving me all the way up there and back. She was a very special friend even if in this case she might have been a little misguided.

I'd decided I would put the whole sorry question of Joe into a locked box in the darkest recess of my mind. It could sit next to the locked box containing Charles and his betrayal – they could stay there together as long as they liked as far as I was concerned.

At breakfast, Reverend Mother rushed into the dining room flapping her hands high over her head.

"Mr Oak has had the most tremendous review in the paper," she said. "The national paper! What a triumph it is for our school, to think that he is on the staff – the parents will be beyond impressed. My goodness, 'a young up-and-coming musician with much to give' – that's how the critic has described him. Look, Flora!"

I took the paper in my trembling hands. Yes, the critic had opened his ears and heard the truth. Joe's performance had been sensational.

"I'm so pleased," I said to Reverend Mother. "It was a great concert and thank you so much for allowing me to have the time off to go up to London. I promise I won't let you down. I'm going to work extra hard now."

"I have no doubt," she said. "You always do, Flora."

Later on that morning, Joe came down to the Music Hut for his teaching. He popped his head round my door wearing dark glasses while I was teaching, which made all the girls laugh.

"Hello!" I said. "Girls! Some of you know Mr Oak. He gave the most incredible concert in London last night. There's a fantastic review in the paper which I've cut out and put on the music board in the corridor. You should have a look on your way out."

"I was blown away by that review," Joe said. "Good, wasn't it?"

"I can't talk at the moment," I said. "Teaching."

"Understood," he said. "Catch up with you later."

I made sure I ran off as soon as the bell went for morning break. I didn't go to the Staff Room but for a long walk in the woods – I couldn't face Joe yet.

I was about to do the same at lunchtime, to sneak off without a word, but he was too quick and rushed into my teaching room.

"Flora! I thought I might have seen you in the foyer last night."

Direct – and to the point.

"It was a shame, because I wanted to introduce you to someone who's very special to me. I've told her so much about you and she's dying to meet you..."

"Sorry," I cut in. "I felt like some fresh air. I saw you come into the foyer and then you looked pretty busy greeting other people. I knew I'd see you today so it didn't really matter. Sorry."

"No problem," Joe said. "I just hope there wasn't anything wrong?"

"It was a beautiful concert," I said. "There must have been so many people there who were proud of you."

"I don't know about that," he said, "but my parents were there, some other family members and loads of friends too. A whole bunch of us went out for a meal afterwards – I can never eat before a concert – and we had quite a few drinks too."

"Yes," I said, "We all noticed the dark glasses."

"In the end," Joe said, "I didn't drive back last night. Too shattered! I stayed with a friend and drove down this morning. Luckily my first pupil wasn't till 10 o'clock."

"That was lucky," I said. "Do you think you'll manage to last until orchestra this afternoon?"

"No problem," he said, "and please don't feel that you have to come to help me. You look rather tired yourself."

"I am," I said. "I might use the time to get on with sifting through the entries for the Carol competition. If you don't mind, maybe I'll sit at the back of the Hall and do my work on a table. That way, if you need me, I'll be close at hand."

"Great," Joe said. "Don't want a repeat of last week's performance, do we? All the girls fancying they were in love with me..."

"They were only pretending," I said. "I hope you know that. It was little more than a silly game to them."

"Of course I knew that," Joe said. "You didn't actually think..."

"Well, people can be strange," I said. "They pretend they like someone when they are already with someone else. That counts as wrong in my book – how about yours?"

I sat far away from Joe at lunch gobbling my

food furiously – then made my excuses, muttering something about carols, and beetled back to the Hut.

Keeping busy was always the answer for me. I would throw myself into my work.

I picked up a few compositions, but they seemed hard to read, blurry, with the notes swimming all over the place. I hoped that Joe wouldn't dare to come into my teaching room after the way I'd spoken to him. He must realise by now what I thought of his behaviour.

"Hi! OK to come in?"

"Joe! What is it?"

"You'll never believe what's happened!" he said. "I've just had a phone call from London. It's so exciting!"

"Really."

Maybe some more people had phoned him to say they were in love with him. Or whatever.

"Yes," he said, "my accompanist from last night rang the school. He had some trouble finding the number but he remembered me saying I worked at St Cecilia's Convent School and found the number in the end. I know it sounds big-headed but he seemed to think I'd played well last night. Anyway, he's due to go on a concert tour with a friend of his tomorrow, but the friend has broken his arm..."

I tapped my pencil on the side of the piano. How long was this going to take? I had compositions to mark.

"And as his friend is a violinist, the upshot is I'm

going to take his place. I can't believe it! It's true what they say – one opportunity leads to another."

"I see. Well, you did have a very good review last night," I said. "Well done again for that. And well done for getting this date."

This was not the date I'd had in mind for Joe.

"So, you'll have to re-organise your teaching again," I said. "Move a few lessons around?"

Joe twisted his mouth. "I think it will require something more radical than that to cover two weeks away in Europe..."

"Two weeks? Europe?" The realisation of the impact this might have on the Christmas concert began to percolate through my tired brain.

"I'll miss two orchestra rehearsals as well as all my teaching," Joe said. "I can take Orchestra tonight but after that you won't be seeing me for over a fortnight. I'm so sorry about this."

He didn't look at all apologetic, but was beaming from ear to ear.

"Have you talked to Sister Barbara?" I said. "Have you realised what this means for the concert and for your pupils?"

"Naturally," Joe said. "I would never have considered this without asking her first, and of course I'm asking you too, then I have to ring my accompanist back immediately and say yes or no."

"What did Sister Barbara say?" I asked.

"She seemed incredibly happy," Joe said. "She said it was a great coup for the school to have a performing musician on the staff and she fully realised that this meant I couldn't always be here. Then she said something about writing an article for the School magazine about my life as a concert violinist – and she invited me to give a masterclass with some of my pupils next term."

I simply couldn't believe how conceited this man was getting. He already seemed to think half the county was in love with him and now he was strutting about, posing as some sort of musical superstar who could waltz off around the world whenever he wanted and leave me to cope with the fall out.

"No way will I leave you in the lurch," Joe said. "I've got a substitute lined up. It's a bit of a commute for her to get here but she's very happy to do it and very experienced."

Marvellous. Another of his women.

"How come she's available," I said, "in the middle of the term?"

"She retired last summer," he said, "after a long career; she's finding she's not enjoying being at home as much as she'd thought and would like to do some teaching again."

"Sounds as if you've got it all sorted out," I said. "Now if you'll excuse me, I should be getting on with these carols."

I sat at a table in the Hall as promised during Orchestra while Joe took the rehearsal. Once I'd had a look through the carols, I made a start on drafting the order of events for the concert. Some of the girls had drawn pictures next to their carols and I thought it would be rather nice if one of these was featured on the front of the programme.

I managed not to gaze at Joe too often, partly because the girls were very sharp-eyed and noticed these things, but also because I was trying to resign myself to the fact that he was never going to be mine.

Susie came into the Hall at the end of the rehearsal to collect Diana and take her home, and I took the opportunity to remember my manners.

"Thank you so much, Susie, for giving me a lift back last night," I said. "I'm so sorry I didn't say anything last night – I was too tired."

And emotional.

"Don't worry," she said. "I completely understand. It was a divine concert though, wasn't it?"

"Yes," I said. "Truly, it was. The music was absolutely stunning. Thank you."

"Joe's a fabulous player," Wendy said as we sat sipping our coffee in the Staff Room two days later.

"Yes, he is." I buried my face in my mug.

"Pass me a squashed fly, will you?" she said. "I'm famished. Aren't you going to ask me how I got on when I went out to dinner?"

"How did you get on when you went out to dinner?"

"I thought you never ask!" she said. "It was great – and it was different."

"Did you go on to a nightclub?" I said. "Did you

get home in the small hours?"

She took a sip of coffee. "No, I didn't. We had a nice quiet meal and talked then I drove home. It was like chatting to a friend – quite a bizarre experience."

I sat up. "What's he like, this new guy?"

"Objectively," she said, "he's not even that good-looking, but I find him strangely attractive. He's so kind and thoughtful." She blushed deeply. "I can't stop thinking about him – it's quite weird."

"You always say you can't stop thinking about someone," I said, "until you think about the next someone..."

"No, you don't understand," she said. "I don't want to think about anyone else or look for anyone else now I've met Richard. He's the one."

I waited. Wendy would usually give me a blow by blow account of a goodnight hug or kiss with a new man.

"If you're expecting any juicy details, well, you're out of luck. He's very shy."

"Wow!" I said. "It's happened to you at last, Wendy. You've fallen in love."

She chuckled. "I do believe you're right. And I'm beginning to understand what all the fuss is about; I've even been thinking about Richard instead of thinking about myself all the time." She took another bite of a biscuit. "You wait until it happens to you again," she said. "It's glorious!"

"Well," I said, "since I know that you're definitely not interested in Joe, I think it's time I told you something. I'm head over heels in love with that man – so much, it hurts."

Wendy's hand froze in the act of reaching for another biscuit. "Tell me all!"

"There's nothing else to tell," I said, "except that I can't stop brooding about him. Although I have to. I need to. It's not the same as for you and Richard – there's a massive complication. Joe is involved with someone else. And my heart is breaking."

Chapter 20

"Now, girls!" Sister Barbara's voice echoed around the Hall. "Another Monday morning, another week ahead of you, another chance to do your best and to remember that you are young ladies."

"Another week nearer the end of term," a girl whispered.

"Yes, closer to going home for Christmas..."

"And getting away from the nuns!"

"Ahem!" Sister Barbara said. "Yes, it is another week closer to the end of term and Christmas but it is also a week closer to the end of term exams."

"Crumbs, I'd forgotten about those," a girl said.

"They don't matter, do they?" another said.

"The school exams are important," Sister Barbara reminded the girls, "because you need to have a reasonably good set of results on your reports – your parents expect it. However, never forget that your main aim is to become cheerful young ladies. Those of you who are more at home on the hockey pitch or in the sewing room are just as important as the brain boxes amongst you. All I ask is that you try your best."

"Thank you, Sister Barbara," Reverend Mother

said. "Now, you may see a special visitor to the school this week – a gentleman who has come all the way from the United States of America. If you happen to see him, remember – you do not stare, you do not point, you do not laugh. You may smile if he speaks to you and you may make the appropriate greeting in return."

"Hank," a girl whispered.

"Yeah! That guy from America."

"Diana told me all about him – he used to go out with her mum!"

"It's awesome, isn't it?"

"Yes! He's been staying with Diana and her mum for a few days already...and that nun, Sister Claire, she's been visiting them..."

"So is it true? About Hank being Sister Claire's father?"

Sister Barbara clapped her hands. "Quiet girls! There's no need to talk."

"I know what Reverend Mother's going to say next..." the whisperer continued.

"So do I..."

"It's what the nuns always say when something exciting happens."

"And girls," Reverend Mother said, "there is no need to mention our special visitor when you write to your parents, is there?"

"See! I knew she'd say that..." the girl muttered.

"Quiet now!" Reverend Mother said. "I have a further important announcement."

"A spaceship's going to land on the hockey pitch

this afternoon?" a cheeky girl suggested.

"I expect we're going to see a film in the gym on Sunday."

"Can't be as bad as the last one."

"Yeah – that was so boring."

"And do you remember, they built it up into something really big and yet..."

"When we got there, it was *The Railway Children*."

"Again. We saw that last term."

"Would you be quiet, girls," Reverend Mother yelled. "Remember, you are young ladies!" She smoothed down the folds of her habit. "I can't think what has got into you all this morning. Now, as some of you who learn the violin already know, Mr Oak is touring the world at the moment. We are extremely lucky to have a teacher of his calibre in the school."

"And I have a special postcard to read you," Sister Barbara said, "from Spain!" She reached inside her pocket, pulling out a shiny dog-eared card and held it above her head, swinging round so that everyone could take a look.

"I'll read it to you now," she said.

Dear everyone at St. Cecilia's, the weather in Madrid is beautifully sunny and I'm looking out at the sea from my hotel balcony. This evening I'm giving a recital with my accompanist. I hope all my pupils are practising hard! Yours, Mr Oak.

"Wasn't that kind of him," Reverend Mother said. "An internationally famous concert violinist touring the world has taken the trouble to write to us."

"Yes, Reverend Mother," the girls chanted obediently.

"Some of you also know that there is a substitute teacher in the school," Reverend Mother said.

"Yes," Sister Barbara said, "she is covering Mr Oak's lessons and the Orchestra rehearsals."

Reverend Mother leant forward, fixing the room with a particularly eagle-eyed glare. "In the past there has been poor behaviour in Orchestra – I do not, repeat, do not want to hear about anything that could ultimately lead to detentions. Have I made myself clear?"

"Yes, Reverend Mother."

Reverend Mother straightened her veil and Sister Barbara said, "I think that is all –have a wonderful week girls. You are dismissed. Miss Gold? If I might have a quick word..."

I stood up from the piano stool and went over to Sister Barbara.

"How are the concert preparations going?" she said. "All fine?"

"No problems at all," I said. "All running smoothly."

"We've decided," Sister Barbara said, "to relieve you of your weekend duties until the end of term. You've got quite enough to do with all the music. How do you feel about that idea?"

"That would be a great help." I said. "I'm still working through Carol entries to choose a winner then we've got to get it rehearsed. Not having to do extra duties and supervise the dormitories means that I could go and stay with my parents for a weekend. Obviously I'd take some work with me, but it would be really nice to see them. Get away for a bit. Thank you."

"Excellent," Sister Barbara said. "That's settled then. You're due some rest and relaxation – just as Hank had here in the War."

I left the Hall feeling very pleased that I would soon be able to go home to Surrey – and also thrilled that Hank was finally going to be coming back to St Cecilia's, where as a young American serviceman he had fallen in love with Susie.

When Susie had phoned Hank the week before, he'd booked a plane ticket immediately and had made his way over to England as fast as he could. And from what I'd heard from Susie so far, the visit was turning out to be a resounding success.

At break time Susie brought Hank into the Staff Room. He was a tall upright figure with thick greying hair and an open friendly face.

"And this is Flora," Susie said as she introduced us.

"Charmed!" Hank bowed and kissed my hand. "I owe you a great deal; Susie told me about everything you did for her and Claire. I find I don't have the words to tell you everything in my heart, but know this: I will forever be grateful to you."

"Come to supper," Susie said to me, "later in the

week. What do you say?"

"Love to," I said, "and it's so good to meet you, Hank."

As Susie proudly introduced Hank to other colleagues, I noticed what a handsome couple they made. Not that they were a couple of course – they hadn't even seen each other for over thirty years before last weekend – and yet I did wonder, like everyone else at St Cecilia's, if perhaps fate had brought them together for a special reason.

I wondered even more when I saw Hank relaxing at the dinner table in Susie's house with Claire on one side of him and Diana on the other. He looked magnificently at home.

"I can't believe it!" he said. "I simply can't believe I'm here with my daughter. Thank you," he said to Claire. "Thank you for persisting, for tracing me, for writing to me, and I'm so sorry I've brought you such a lot of trouble." He put his head down. "That Grace – she really is a mixed-up woman. She's finding it hard to accept that she is no longer a significant person in my life – and never will be again. She always was very possessive – quite an eccentric character."

"Is there any news of her?" I said. "I haven't heard anything since she was taken away by the police that night in the Music Hut."

"She's safety locked up," Hank said, "and by that I mean that you're safe from her, also that she's safe from herself. She's having some sort of psychiatric treatment, I believe. I hope she'll be transferred back to the States soon, because, no disrespect ladies, but I believe that sort of thing is more advanced in the U S of A than it is over here."

"Yes," Claire said, "and as I've said before, I think Grace is more sad than bad."

No one said anything for a minute. Hearing about another's inability to cope with reality always gives pause for thought – and, in my case, a choked-up feeling.

"Pudding?" Susie said eventually.

"I sure love your English puddings," Hank said. "I remember them from when I stayed at St Cecilia's in the War. Us boys all loved those desserts – sponge pudding, blancmange, apple pie – no end to them! And the stewed fruit as well, prunes, rhubarb, plums, with lashings of custard..."

"Have you shown Hank the graffiti down in the Undercroft?" I asked Susie.

"She sure has!" Hank said. "It was great to see reminders of my friends down there as well." He looked down at the table and frowned. "Some of those friends didn't make it through the War. I guess I was one of the lucky ones."

"Let's not be gloomy," Susie said. "Let's make the most of the time we have."

"Sure thing," Hank said. "I'll be back in the States all too soon."

"Well, I hope you're staying for the Christmas Concert," I said.

"When's that?" he asked.

"Beginning of December," I said. "Not long, as I keep telling the girls."

Hank looked across the table at Susie and she said, "I'd love you to stay on. You're welcome here as long as you want."

"Well, I don't have anyone to get back for," Hank said. "Work say I can stay as long as I need to – they owe me a great deal of holiday because I never take my full allowance. So yes, I'd be delighted to stay for the Christmas Concert."

"That's settled then," Claire said. "And I'm definitely staying till the concert because I'm singing in it." She looked round the room at Susie and Claire and also at Hank. "I'll be going home at the end of term, back to Rome – and I hope very soon my new family will come out and see me. All of you."

"Cool! I love travelling," Diana said.

"Have you travelled much?" Hank asked.

"I've visited Weston-Super-Mare," Diana said, "on a school geography trip. I went to Scotland once and I've been to Salisbury quite a few times."

Hank slapped his thighs. "You must all come out to the States and see me. I'd love it!"

Claire gave me a lift back to St Cecilia's at the end of the evening. I couldn't help remembering the last time I had taken this route with Joe in his Mini.

"Penny for them?" Claire said.

"No, it's nothing," I replied.

"Thinking about Joe," she asked, "and the last time you were at Susie's?"

"That's right," I said.

"Sometimes things have a funny way of working out," she said. "I mean, look at me! When I started looking for my parents, first of all I had no idea if I would find them, then I didn't know whether they would want to see me."

"It didn't work out completely smoothly though, did it?" I said. "Don't forget about Grace."

"True," Claire said. "She is quite an unusual character, I must say. I feel sorry for her. She's totally overcome with jealousy and obviously rather unstable."

"And you're a very kind lady," I said. "Lots of people would bear her a grudge after what she's put you through."

"I've learnt not to think like that," Claire said. "Life's too short."

"Do you think Susie bears a grudge?" I asked. "I mean, what do you think she feels about Hank?"

"No, she definitely doesn't blame him for anything," Claire said. "As to what she feels about him, I'm not sure. Hank didn't know she was pregnant when he left. He's talked to us about it a lot, got quite upset actually. He said he'd wanted to stay in England, but as a young serviceman he had no control over where he went. He was sent back to the States with the rest of his friends – I think they had about six hours' notice."

"Totally different world," I said.

"Very intense," Claire said. "We can't judge it by our standards; we have no idea what it felt like to live through the War. Rightly or wrongly, Hank and Susie were parted by circumstances and didn't manage to keep in contact."

"So sad." I said.

"Yes," Claire agreed. "Hank said when he got back to the States, it took him ages to get over his wartime experiences – it affected him very deeply. After quite a few years, he tried to find out what had happened to Susie. One of his friends was living in England by then, not far from Salisbury, and he asked him to see if he could find out if Susie was still at St. Cecilia's."

"What happened when he found she was still there?" I said.

"Nothing," Claire said, "because Hank's friend also found out that Susie was engaged to be married by then, to Bob, her late husband. Hank didn't want to spoil anything for her. He said if she was in love with someone and was engaged to be married, that's all he wanted. He put her happiness before his own – and that's quite something. I'm so proud of my father for that."

"I still don't understand why Susie hadn't told him she was pregnant."

"She was very young and didn't realise for ages," Claire said, "by which time Hank had been sent back to the States. I think for a long time she probably didn't want to admit even to herself that there was a baby on the way – and I think too that she didn't have the confidence to contact Hank. It was all very different in those days."

"Yes, another era completely," I said. "What is it they say? The past is a foreign country..."

"It was Reverend Mother who ultimately helped her rebuild her life," Claire said. "Susie says Reverend Mother was a tower of strength and she wouldn't have known what to do if it hadn't been for the kindness she received from her, in fact from all the nuns."

"Reverend Mother is a very special person," I said. "She's helped me a lot in the past year. If it's not an odd thing to say, she has a strong maternal instinct."

"Yes, she does," Claire said. "She's been incredibly friendly and welcoming to me. I love being in the convent here; you know, for two pins I'd transfer permanently from Rome to St Cecilia's."

"What!" I said. "You'd leave the sunshine and all that delicious Italian food – and come and live in Dorset with the rain, not to mention the rissoles and baked beans."

"It sounds mad, I know," Claire said, "but I am seriously considering it. Please don't say anything to Susie and Diana yet, or Hank. Of course, it wouldn't be for some time especially because I've promised them a holiday in Rome, but there's nothing like family, is there? And there's the added bonus that I'd be so much nearer to visit my other parents in Northamptonshire."

"You have a positive embarrassment of parents," I said. "You are one lucky lady!"

"Yes, I am!" she said. "Now, we just need to get

you sorted out. You've been working too hard, I think. You need a break."

"Well, I am going to stay with my parents this weekend."

"You don't sound totally delighted, if you don't mind me saying."

I sighed. "It can be difficult. I don't know how much you know about me?"

"Susie has told me a few things," Claire said. "She hasn't gossiped but she's mentioned you'd had a Disappointment."

"A Disappointment is a good description," I said. "Disappointment with a capital D. You see the thing is, every time I go and stay with my parents, I'm always scared that Charles, he's my ex, will be staying in the village and I don't want to see him. Ever again. He married one of my friends I'd been at school with. Her parents still live in the village, near my parents – and her parents are Charles' in-laws."

"I see," Claire said.

"And it's a very small village."

"Is there no way you could resolve the situation?" Claire suggested. "Sort it out once and for all?"

"I should have a go, shouldn't I?"

If only I could work out how.

Chapter 21

"Hello Dad! It's so kind of you to pick me up from the station."

My father took my grip and stowed it in the boot of his car.

"Lovely to see you sweetheart!" he said. "You don't come and see us often enough – we're always saying that."

"Dad!" I said indignantly. "I am a grown up. I have my own life!"

"Yes, I know," he said. "It's just that we miss you. Our nest is empty – sometimes we simply don't know what to do with ourselves."

"That's such an exaggeration," I said. "You're always busy – with your garden, your friends and the village activities, not to mention amateur dramatics. I won't be able to get that magnificent performance of *The Pirates of Penzance* out of my mind in a hurry. It was fabulous!"

My father started whistling the tune of *I Am the Very Model of a Modern Major-General* while I clapped along and sang,

"*...I've information vegetable, animal and mineral...*"

I felt a powerful sense of relief as I walked in the front door and saw my mother standing there in the kitchen in her apron, her hands flowery from rolling out pastry and a fragrant sponge cake on the side. It was brilliant to be home.

"What's with the bulging music case?" Mum said. "Thought you were supposed to be having a relaxing weekend?"

"I will be relaxing," I said, "but I need to run through a few of these carols. The competition's more popular than ever this year and I've still got about twenty carols I haven't even looked at. I'll be playing them through on the piano later, if you're interested."

"I'm sure they're all splendid," Dad said, "and I look forward to hearing them. Now, your mother's made your favourite meal. Must be starving after that long journey. Sit down."

After supper I unpacked my few belongings and then went downstairs to sit with my parents.

"Don't let us cramp your style," Dad said. "If you want to pop to the pub and see if any of your friends are there, feel free."

"No," I said, "I came home to see you. Besides, most of my friends have moved away."

"Yes," Dad said. "The average age of the village residents does seem to be quite high at the moment."

"But some of our friends have their children to visit," Mum said, "and then inevitably, those children marry and have their own children too. So many of our friends are becoming grandparents."

There was a sudden chill in the room and my mother looked at me. "I didn't mean to be tactless," she said. "Sorry."

"You don't have to protect me, Mum," I said. "I've got over Charles."

"I'm glad you know about it," she said. "I didn't want to be the one to tell you."

"Tell me what?" I said.

"So you didn't know?" she said. "Oh dear, well..."

"What Mum is trying to tell you," Dad said, "is that Charles and his wife are expecting. I heard last week at a rehearsal in the village hall. Apparently there's a baby arriving in the spring."

I turned in soon after that. Not much point in sitting up any longer when I felt so tired. And I wanted to be on my own and process the news. It wasn't that surprising – people who are married do have babies, after all – but somehow it made it much more final.

Before I got into bed, I rummaged around in the top drawer of my dressing table and pulled out a small box. Opening it, I looked at the sparkling ring inside, the ring Charles had given me when we had become engaged.

I had thought about returning it many times, but didn't want to give the ring back in front of other people and wasn't ready to see him on my own. Too painful. I had once thought of going around to his in-laws to give them the ring, but that would have been crazy. Perhaps I could have posted it, but it was a valuable ring and I didn't want it to go astray. So many excuses...

In books, when an engagement fails, the woman generally throws the ring at her fiancé. I couldn't have thrown my ring at Charles because he'd broken the news on the phone, coward that he was.

I slipped the ring onto my finger one last time, promising myself that I would find a way to get rid of it. Maybe I could donate it to charity? Give it to a beggar in the street? Not many beggars in our village, but still...

The ring was far too big for my finger because I'd lost tons of weight over the previous year. I was a different person now.

It was a wide gold band with a big flashy diamond. I'd never liked it although I'd been proud to wear it because I had loved Charles so much. He'd presented me with the ring one day shortly after he asked me to marry him, saying that if I didn't like it he could change it, no bother. I thought I shouldn't say what I felt – that I would have liked a smaller ring, maybe an antique, rather than the self-important stone he had chosen. I could see straight away it would be a nuisance when I played the piano, but I wanted to please him and so kept quiet.

I put the ring back in its box and went over to the side where there was an old pencil case. Taking out a tiny roll of sticky tape, I sealed the edge of the box. I would never open it again – moreover I would give the ring back to Charles on the next possible occasion.

On Saturday morning Mum and I walked through the village. She wanted to buy some fruit and bread and then we thought we'd go out for a coffee. One of her friends ran a little teashop and we sat there over drinks and scones, looking out at the ducks on the village pond. It was as if time had stood still. St Cecilia's could have been a thousand miles away, and thoughts of Joe, Susie, my work, all of it, didn't cross my mind. I was home.

"Look!" Mum said. "Look behind the counter! There are all sorts of cakes for sale. Let's go over there now and choose some."

"We don't need to do that, Mum," I said. "I saw you'd been baking last night when I arrived. You've got enough cakes at home to sink a battleship."

"No, quick," she said. "You need to come and look at these cakes immediately."

I wondered what was going on but I picked up my bag and started to walk to the back of the café.

"Yes, Mum, that is a scrumptious looking Victoria sponge," I said, "but you have an even nicer one in the tin at home."

"Never mind," she said. "I think we can go now."

As we came out of the shop she said, "This way – no, let's go to the left, come on, quickly..."

We went into the wool shop on the corner. Mum was a great knitter, always looking for new projects.

"I thought you might like a new cardigan, Flora,"

she said. "I need something to do to keep me occupied when your father's out singing in the evenings with his Gilbert and Sullivan group."

"OK," I said. "Thank you."

Inside the shop, Mum busied herself flicking through patterns at the counter while I looked at the beautiful displays of wool in the window. I was particularly drawn to a vibrant flecked mixture of beautiful autumn colours – or should I choose the bright blues and reds? So tricky to decide.

My hand flew to my mouth when I saw Charles with his bride – my ex-fiancé with my former friend. They were walking hand-in-hand on the other side of the road and she was wearing a smock top underneath her unbuttoned coat. They both had that goofy expression parents-to-be wear – off on a planet of their own, full of hope and excitement. No wonder Mum had tried to keep me away from them.

"So, what shall we do this evening?" my father said after supper. "Television, card game, piano duets – what do you fancy?"

"You know yesterday," I said, "you mentioned I might like to go to the pub? Well, I think I will tonight, if you don't mind. It's my last chance because I'll be back in Dorset tomorrow. I'd like to see if any of my old friends are there. I won't be more than half an hour."

"Jolly good idea!" my father said. "They can't all have moved away."

"Are you absolutely sure?" my mother said.
Did she suspect I had a plan in mind?
"Yes – I'm sure it's what I want to do."

The pub smelt of stale smoke and spilt beer. Pop music blared from a speaker in the corner, dried hops hung from the beamed ceiling and a roaring fire crackled in the grate. Nothing had changed since I'd first visited as a teenager with my friends from school. We thought it was so cool then, to be in the grown ups' territory.

I saw Charles straight away, sitting on his own in the corner nursing a pint. My father had once told me that when Charles and his wife stayed in the village, he'd often seen Charles in the pub on his own, obviously giving his new bride time alone with her parents.

Charles narrowed his eyes when I walked over to his table.

"Mind if I sit down?" I said.

"Flora," he said. "It's been a long time."

"I don't want to rake up the past," I said. "I want to draw a line under it and I can't yet because this is yours."

I plonked the ring box in front of him.

He stared. "You don't have to give that back, not after what I did."

"Not after you betrayed me and dumped me?"

He looked down. "I'm sorry."

My heart started pounding. This was the first time he had ever said he was sorry. For anything.

"I realise now I behaved contemptibly," he said.

"What's done is done," I said. "You can't change the past."

"I don't want to change the past," he said. "I think splitting up was the right decision. We weren't suited; no honestly, you should be with someone who understands you, probably a musician, truth be told. We wouldn't have worked, Flora. I'm saying sorry for the way I did it. I should have talked to you face-to-face, been honest. I was a selfish bastard and I apologise unreservedly."

"Thank you," I whispered. "That means a lot."

Charles put his hand over mine. "It must have been a huge shock for you and I'm more sorry for my behaviour than I can ever express."

I looked into his eyes, but Charles was no longer the man I had been engaged to, the man of my dreams. He didn't look like the man of my nightmares either, which is how I had been thinking of him recently. He was just an ordinary person who had found himself in a situation he'd wanted to get out of and couldn't think of a graceful way to do it.

"I mean it," he said. "You should keep the ring."

"I mean it too. I don't want your ring. Sell it back to the jewellers and buy something for the new baby, OK?"

I stood up and folded my scarf around my neck ready for the cold. "Best wishes to your family."

"Yours too," Charles said.

I walked the long way round the village back to

Mum and Dad's, feeling like a real grown up for once. I'd never be scared to come home again. It wouldn't matter if Charles and his family were there, it wouldn't matter one little fig, because that chapter of my life was over.

I could see now it was a good thing that Charles and I had split up. We weren't suited. And Charles, although he might have gone about it the wrong way, had been brave enough to end the relationship.

And what about the future? I looked up to the sky. So many more stars here than when I had gazed into the London sky after Joe's concert; they were twinkling and winking, sending me messages of hope. Whatever happened now, I knew I would be able to deal with it. My heart had definitely recovered and I was ready to get back in the ring at last.

Chapter 22

Life was different once I got back to school after staying with my parents, especially since Joe was still abroad on tour. I was able to focus whole-heartedly on the job in hand, getting everything ready for the all-important St. Cecilia's Christmas Concert. Every morning I sprang out of bed full of purpose, anxious to get on with another rehearsal, another carol, another descant to learn.

Sister Claire became a real asset in the choir; she had omitted to mention before that she sang in the chapel choir at her convent in Rome and also played the organ and sometimes conducted the other nuns. We ended up doing St Cecilia's choir as a sort of double act; she played the piano while I conducted. She was not only a tremendous help but was fast becoming a close friend too.

As the days rolled past I was delighted to see Hank spending more time at St. Cecilia's. I often saw him walking with Susie in the grounds. One day, Diana had exciting news to share in her music lesson.

"You'll never guess what, Miss Gold!" she said, eyes shining.

"I don't think I will be able to guess – with all the extraordinary things that have been happening over the past few weeks, I can't imagine what's coming next."

"Well," Diana said, "Hank, Mum and me, we're all going to Rome for Christmas to visit Claire. Isn't it fabulous? I can't wait! My friend are so jealous."

"Super!" I said. "I know that you'll all have an amazing time."

I put my fingers behind my back and crossed them, hoping that something extra special would be happening for Susie and Hank. Susie had enjoyed a wonderful marriage with Bob her husband but now he was gone and I could see she was growing fonder of Hank every day.

As for him, from the very beginning Hank had seemed completely besotted with Susie. The fact that he'd never managed to find another woman to hold a candle to her told its own tale.

"Are you all right, Miss Gold?" Diana said. "Should I continue playing my composition to you?"

"Oh yes, go ahead," I said. "Sorry! I was busy thinking about what a heavenly time you're going to have in Italy. Lucky you!"

As Diana picked out the chords of her latest composition, I felt cheered as I reflected how love can triumph in adversity. Who would have thought the romance that had started so long ago between two teenagers would flower again all these years later? It defied belief.

I put my head down. Maybe a love story would come true for me someday. I knew that Joe had someone else in his life and I would have to get used to the fact that he was unavailable. Given time I might even feel able to meet the glamorous blonde with a turned-up nose who had flung herself into his arms after his Wigmore Hall recital.

Would there be someone else out there for me?

Joe continued to send postcards, cataloguing all the places he was visiting. Vienna, Florence, Paris – he was having a whirlwind tour.

One Friday morning in Assembly, Reverend Mother read his latest communication to the enraptured girls.

"...and so, girls, Mr Oak will be in school today," she said. "He is due back this morning. Now, as it is Friday and our flute teacher is also in, if you are expecting a lesson with Mr Oak, you should report to the Blue Parlour. Violin lessons have been moved there for the day."

No one in the Hall appeared to be listening; they had all run to the bay window and the air was positively crackling with excitement.

"He's here now!"

"Look out of the window! There's his Mini!"

"Mr Oak! Mr Oak!"

"He's so tanned!"

"How did he have time to sunbathe?"

Reverend Mother didn't seem to have the heart to reprimand the girls but instead ran over to the window herself.

"He's here! He's here!" she shrieked before beetling to the Entrance Hall and flinging open the door. Whatever it was she said to Joe as he got out of his car, it made him grin, and he kissed her hand. When she smiled and pointed to the Hall window, he waved to all the girls with their noses pressed against the pane.

I stayed sitting at the piano in the Hall drumming my heels on the ground. Then I straightened my spine. I was determined to keep going and cope with whatever I had to face.

When I reached the Music Hut, Wendy was already there waiting for her pupils.

"He's back," she said.

"Who?" I asked.

"Joe, of course," she said. "I hope he comes down to say hello before he starts teaching."

"Hello ladies!" a voice at the door said. "I bring presents from my travels – greetings from the continent!"

Joe put the most enormous box of sumptuous looking liquor chocolates on the table.

"This will help us get through the last few days before the Christmas Concert," he said.

"Wow!" Wendy said. "I adore chocolates! Thank you so much."

She flew across the room and gave him a massive hug.

"Yes, thank you," I said.

Joe grinned and I wondered if he would expect a hug from me as well. I quickly positioned myself behind the piano so that it wasn't an option.

"How were the concerts?" I asked.

"Oh, fabulous," he said. "We had a whale of a time, but it's great to be home again."

"I thought you said you liked living out of a suit-case?" I teased.

He put his head on one side. "Maybe I'm getting to appreciate home more. In fact, the way I'm feel-ing at the moment, if I never see another airport in my life, it won't bother me at all. However much fun you have away, it's always a relief to get home. Home is where the heart is."

"Oh, yes," Wendy said. "I travel quite a lot myself and I'm always relieved to get back. That moment when you chuck your case in the corner and slip your shoes off..."

"Talking of home," Joe said, "the most marvel-lous opportunity has come up." He turned to me. "Remember I said I was looking for somewhere to live? I love staying with my parents but it's time I had my own place. Well, I've found a beautiful cottage to rent. I made some enquiries before I left and now with the money I've made from the tour, I can manage the deposit."

"Great," Wendy said. "Where is it?"

"That's the best part," Joe said. "The cottage is right next to the edge of St Cecilia's estate. I'll be able to get to work here in minutes every morning – in fact I could walk through the woods and not bring the car."

"I think if you don't bring your Mini to work," I said, "Reverend Mother and all the girls will be inconsolable. They worship that car."

"I adore her too," Joe said. "My pride and joy. Anyway, the point is, I'm having a painting weekend – planning to decorate from top to bottom. The cottage is in a bit of a state and needs freshening up. Got some paint charts here somewhere in my bag – thought you might want to look at them, Flora. Help me choose some colours."

There was a sharp intake of breath from Wendy – I was mightily surprised too.

"I'm not sure why you think I'd be any good at choosing colours," I said, "or why you would even want me to."

"Just an idea," he said. "Thought you'd be interested. Anyway I'm inviting you both over at the weekend whenever you feel like it. There'll be tons of people there. I'm supplying paint brushes, rollers, all that sort of stuff."

"And wine?" Wendy asked.

"Sure," Joe said. "Absolutely essential! What about it, Flora. Fancy popping over?"

"Well I'm going to," Wendy said. "May I bring my friend Richard with me?"

"Of course," Joe said. "The more the merrier. Flora? You need a break from your concert preparations."

"OK," I said.

"Brilliant!" Joe rubbed his hands together in delight. “And do you know what? Reverend Mother and Sister Barbara said they might turn up as well. They’re going to bring some sandwiches from the school kitchen.”

“Oh dear,” I said.

“Yes, that sounds disastrous,” Wendy said. “What if I bring some food? I’m not sure anyone wants to eat school sandwiches.”

And so it was that I found myself making my way through the woods on Saturday afternoon wearing my oldest clothes to help Joe.

The cottage was about half a mile from the school. I’d often passed quite near when out on one of my woodland walks and had wondered if anyone lived there. I had never seen any smoke rising from the chimney, not any other signs of habitation. The garden was very over grown – I could see a glimpse of the rough stones of the building through the foliage.

When I arrived at the cottage gate, leaning wonkily half off its hinges, there were several cars parked outside and pounding music coming from the open front door. I rang the bell but no one answered so I stepped inside.

“Hey, Flora!” Joe said. “Welcome!”

“Gosh, that colour’s very bright,” I said, looking at the hall wall that Joe was painting.

“Your choice,” he said, “from yesterday.”

Joe had insisted on showing me his paint charts at lunch time the previous day, asking me what

I liked. I had pointed to orange, coral pink and a very warm yellow. Now he seemed to have taken my word as gospel and was decorating his house in some of my favourite colours.

"Do you think they look a bit too bright?" I said. "Almost too positive?"

"You can't be too positive," he said. "It's impossible!"

He stood back and regarded his handiwork then scratched his head. "I think, anyway!"

We both burst into fits of laughter then a friend of Joe's appeared from the kitchen holding a kettle. "Anyone want a brew?"

"Yes please!" I said. "Now, tell me where to start, Joe."

"Why don't you paint next to me," he said, "here, in the hall? Some of my family are upstairs doing the bedrooms and there are a few friends tackling the sitting room. We'll get it all done in no time at this rate."

"Hello!" Wendy's voice echoed behind us. "Reporting for duty with Richard – my boyfriend, Richard."

I turned around, keen to see this man who seemed to have done the impossible – stolen Wendy's heart. I almost did a double take. Mousey hair, brown spectacles, slim to the point of skinny, diffident and shy-looking, but blessed with one of the kindest faces I had ever seen. Wendy slipped her hand in his and the pair exchanged such a tender look, I felt quite overcome.

On second thoughts – he was probably perfect for her. What is it they say about the attraction of opposites?

After about half an hour, a shout came from upstairs. "Hey Joe! Any chance of a cup of tea up here? Absolutely parched!"

"I'll have to boil some water," he called up. "We seem to have drained the pot already..."

"I'll put the kettle on," I said. "You're right in the middle of doing that strip of wall."

"OK," he said. "Sink's straight through, at the back."

I padded into the kitchen which was pretty much of a wreck. I recognised the convent sandwiches on the side straight away. They were stacked high on a metal tray and made with margarine, bright yellow cheddar and the soft white pappy bread we all called 'Mother's Shame' instead of 'Mother's Pride'. Apparently Reverend Mother and Sister Barbara had been at the cottage this morning bringing sustenance and helping with the gloss paint work around the window frames. They really were troopers, the pair of them – do anything for anyone.

I filled the kettle, desperately trying not to get orange paint on the stainless steel. Then I heard feet coming downstairs and she was in the room. Joe's girlfriend. Her long blonde hair was fastened in a thick plait down her back and her upturned nose looked as cute as ever. Now she was close, I had the opportunity to see her big round blue eyes, beautifully made up with matching blue mascara and eyeshadow. She was stunning.

"Hello," she said. "Flora! It's great to meet you. I think I saw you at Joe's concert. He's told me so much about you. He loves working at St. Cecilia's. Thank you for giving him such a great job there..."

Suddenly I couldn't stand it anymore. I'd had enough of thinking it was OK for Joe to be with someone else. It wasn't fair. I wanted him for myself. I loved him, for God's sake! I absolutely adored the man – worshipped the very bones of him.

Picking up my painting brush, I said, "Could you make the tea? I don't feel terribly well – if you wouldn't mind telling Joe I've gone..."

As I ran out of the kitchen, through the passageway and hall, and out of the front door, I heard Joe's voice.

"Flora! What is it? Where you going – what's wrong? Please don't leave. I wanted to introduce you to my..."

I put my head down as I ran, not wanting to hear anything he said. I had thought I could be friends with Joe, but it wasn't possible. I couldn't bear seeing him with someone else.

It was only when I was halfway back to the convent I realised I still had the brush in my hand, dripping orange paint onto the roots and leaves in the wood.

Chapter 23

The noise in the Blue Parlour was deafening.

"Girls!" I shouted. "Calm down! You'll be on in a minute. Quickly and quietly, no chattering. Remember to stay standing up until the whole Orchestra is assembled, and then sit on my signal."

As a very great privilege, we were allowed to use the Blue Parlour as the green room for concerts; it was much nearer to the Hall than the Music Hut and I appreciated being able to line the girls up there before an event, although I was always anxious about how untidy they might leave the room.

I picked up a programme from the floor, reading, "Wednesday 1st of December 1976. St Cecilia's Christmas Carol Concert..." A picture of a robin perched on a shepherd's crook decorated the front page.

It was finally here.

The last few days had been what I imagined purgatory must be like. I refused to think any more about my journey from Joe's cottage on Sunday back to Slum Alley – how I had thrown all my paint-stained clothes onto the floor and flung myself on my bed weeping.

Now his paintbrush had been cleaned and was hidden away in a drawer in my room. I would return it to him at some point, but never again would I let my guard down and try to be friends with a man who was attached to another. It didn't work.

"Miss Gold," a girl said, "one of my violin strings has snapped and I don't have a spare one."

Sister Claire stepped forward. "Don't worry, dear," she said. "Mr Oak is in the Hall. I'll go and get him – see if he can help."

Within seconds Joe was fixing a new string to the girl's violin.

"Your habit!" I said to Sister Claire. "You're wearing a new habit! The Order of St Cecilia's uniform..."

"Yes!" She gave a proud twirl. "All the nuns have been helping me to stitch this in the evenings. I will be officially joining St Cecilia's after the Christmas break – after my last trip to Rome, with my new family! I'll be teaching Italian to the girls in the New Year, and between you and me, I have ambitions to sort out the school kitchen. No more baked beans and rissoles at the convent from 1977 onwards, that's the aim!"

"A great New Year's Resolution!" I said, giving Sister Claire a massive hug, then I spun round to address the room. "Only a few minutes before we go on, girls. Line up now, quietly please."

"Flora," Joe said urgently into my ear. "Flora! Please, we need to talk..."

"Not now!" I said. "We're about to start."

"Fine, but afterwards."

Wendy waved from the other side of the room and gave me a thumbs up sign. "It's going to be an amazing concert!" she mouthed over the racket.

"Thank you!" I mouthed back.

She seemed to be saying something else. About a mistake? I couldn't make it out. Oh dear. I do hope she hadn't changed her mind about Richard. They had seemed to be getting on so well together.

My heart was practically leaping out of my chest with extra adrenaline. The Christmas Carol Concert represented a vast amount of work – there were so many different items and so much to keep tabs on. I stood tall. It was under control. I could do it!

Sister Barbara rushed into the room and patted my arm. "I have high hopes the concert tonight will be even better than the Christmas Concert last year."

No pressure then.

We processed into the Hall and the orchestra and choir took their places, their ranks swelled by staff and parents, including the taxi driver and his wife. Sister Claire took her place at the piano and arranged her music on the stand for the opening choir item. It was going to be fine. I turned to face the front while Sister Barbara greeted the audience.

"Ladies and gentlemen, welcome to our Christmas Carol Concert. If you haven't been to a concert at St. Cecilia's before tonight, believe me, you're in for a real treat. The girls have been working tirelessly under Miss Gold's direction and with the help of our instrumental staff. The choir is made up of pupils plus many staff, parents and nuns. There's always room for more singers, so if by the end of the concert you're feeling inspired, don't be shy, but make yourself known to Miss Gold. She'll be only too happy to sign you up to sing with us; I believe she has some very splendid plans for the Easter Concert next term involving Handel's *Messiah*."

I smiled, feeling my heart sink somewhat at the thought of all the work that was going to have to be done for that concert. Might be better to get this one over first...

The evening started with *Once in Royal*. Diana sang the solo verse, while Susie wiped away a tear, then I held my hands up high to bring in the full choir and audience. Sister Claire accompanied on the piano, together with a small string ensemble which included Joe on his violin. I tried my hardest not to look at him.

Next Wendy conducted the Wind Group in a medley of Christmas carols while I sat at the side. The parents in the audience had a great time, as did the nuns, tapping their feet and humming along until the Hall was vibrating with the melodies, almost from beneath the floorboards to the rafters. The whole time, Wendy's boyfriend Richard gazed at her with immense pride.

Joe's girlfriend was sitting in the very back row,

her bright blond hair shinning like a halo. My fingers dug into the sides of my legs. Not now, not ever. I didn't want to feel this bitter bleakness again.

Jealousy was a terrible thing. The nuns were always mentioning it – one of the very deadliest sins. I took a deep breath. If I really cared for Joe, I'd be happy for him, just as Hank had tried to be happy for Susie when he'd found out that she was engaged to Bob. I looked down, feeling that I was probably far too selfish to rejoice in Joe's happiness with his girlfriend. I needed to try to be a better person.

The couple next to Joe's girlfriend were older – and resembled her. Maybe her parents? There was another man there too, his shoulder snuggled up against Joe's girlfriend with two small children sitting next to him. An image of the Blue Parlour swam into my head...funny the way the mind worked when you were stressed.

I quickly leafed through the programme on my knee. I needed to check what the next item was. Ah yes, a choir piece. Just a quick look at the music, to check the tempo...

I ticked off item after item on my programme as the concert danced forwards.

String group – tick.

Junior choir – tick.

Recorder Ensemble – tick.

Runners up from the Carol Competition – tick.

And then the interval.

Back in the Blue Parlour, I said to the girls, "Deal with your instruments and then you may go and speak to your parents in the Entrance Hall. Be careful how you put everything away – remember last year when someone put their foot through a cello because it was left abandoned on the floor? It's worth taking an extra bit of time."

I followed the girls to where Reverend Mother and Sister Barbara were standing behind a trestle table serving mince pies and non-alcoholic mulled wine.

"Simply superb!" a parent's voice could be heard saying.

"Excellent! Even better than last year..." another gushed.

"Did you see that new violin teacher playing behind the girls in the first carol?"

"Yes indeed! Apparently he's been touring the world and came back especially for this."

"He teaches my daughter and she's heading for a high distinction in her next exam..."

"I wonder if he's got space for any new pupils..."

"The music staff here are amazing!"

"But none of them are as amazing as Miss Gold – because she keeps them all in order. She's got everything under control..."

If only I did have everything under control, in particular my own heart which seemed to be treacherously searching the room for Joe and his girlfriend.

"I don't want to worry you," Susie said, as I

squeezed past her and her new family.

"Worry me?" I said. "What is it?"

"Sister Claire has just answered a call from the police."

"Yes," Hank said. "Apparently Grace escaped this afternoon – she was being taken for some medical treatment in Salisbury..."

"And somehow managed to give the prison officers the slip," Susie said.

"I'm sure there's nothing to worry about," I said. "She surely wouldn't come back here?"

Hank clenched his teeth. "I'm so sorry to have brought this woman into your lives. If it hadn't been for..."

"Hush now," Susie said. "Everything will be fine. And look, Flora. Joe's beckoning you – see, over there?"

I spotted Joe and his girlfriend standing by the fireplace.

All at once my face flamed red as I recollected the first time I had seen Joe in the Entrance Hall standing in the same place, shortly before he'd been interviewed in the Blue Parlour. The Blue Parlour! Now when had I thought about that recently? Ah yes, during the concert when I'd seen...

Joe was waving frantically at me, desperately trying to get me to go over to him. In a flash it came to me – I remembered how during his interview in the Blue Parlour, Joe had explained how he'd moved down from Yorkshire and how much he was enjoying living with his parents again –

especially because his sister lived nearby with her family.

I looked at the woman standing next to him; I had thought she was his girlfriend but now I could see the resemblance – and those must be his parents standing right by him. As well as hers! There were two small children tugging at his arms – surely Joe was their uncle and the other man could be his brother-in-law...

I floated over to Joe on a cushion of hope. The final piece of the puzzle was, of course, that it wasn't surprising that his sister was one of his accompanists. After all, musicality runs in families.

"Flora," Joe said, "please allow me to introduce my sister."

"Hello," she said. "We did sort of meet in the kitchen on Saturday at Joe's cottage. Sorry you had to rush away so quickly – I hope you're feeling all right now."

"I thought you were..."

"What did you think?" Joe said. "You surely didn't..."

"Yes," Wendy said, joining our group arm in arm with Richard. "Flora thought your sister was your girlfriend."

"Fire!" a voice screamed. "It's in the Undercroft!"

"There's smoke all over the Hall!" a girl cried.

"Outside everyone!" Reverend Mother said. "Quickly!"

"I'll ring the Fire Brigade," Sister Barbara said, haring off towards the Nuns' Quarters.

Reverend Mother led the audience and girls outside, while Joe ran back into the Hall, yelling over his shoulder, "I need to see if there's anyone left in there!"

I raced after him, determined to protect my pupils. And be at his side.

"Flora," he said, choking slightly, "you don't need to be here."

"We have to get down to the Undercroft," I said, "in case some of the girls are trapped there. They might have been on their way to the Music Hut during the interval; we can't take any chances."

"You're right," he said. "We can't wait for the fire brigade – it's going to take too long for them to get here."

He held my hand as we made our way across the Hall and down the narrow staircase to the Undercroft. There, we saw a figure crouched on the ground sobbing, surrounded by burning papers. Joe grabbed the fire extinguisher from the wall and put out the flames.

"Not as bad as it looked," he said. "Paper must have been damp to produce all that smoke."

"Grace!" I said. "What are you doing here?"

She looked up at me, her red-rimmed eyes wild and despairing.

"I don't really know," she said. "I've been in a sort of hospital but today I wanted to come back." She started to beat her fists on the floor. "I wanted to hurt Hank – he should be mine and if it wasn't for Claire writing to him I'm sure he and I would have got back together. Now he's got his own family over here in England, it's never going to happen."

"What were you burning?" Joe asked.

"Letters," Grace said. "After I was arrested, I wrote Hank lots and lots of letters telling him how much I loved him, how I didn't want to let him go. This evening I've been hiding here, listening to the music from the Hall. I even hummed along to some of the carols."

"I heard that!" I said. "Coming up through the floorboards. I never dreamt..."

Grace shook her head. "My plan was to find Hank later – but then I saw this and remembered him saying he had always loved Susie." She jabbed an angry finger at the graffiti where Hank had declared his love for Susie all those years ago. "I realised Hank didn't deserve my love. I had to burn my letters."

"We need to get out of here," I said. "It might not have been a big fire, but smoke carries its own dangers."

Grace coughed as we lifted her to her feet, helping her out of the side door, past the Hut and round the back of the Hall. As we reached safety, a fleet of fire engines, ambulances and police cars whooshed past nosily, parking haphazardly over the top of the drive.

"Somehow I don't think Reverend Mother's going to mind about the untidy parking today," I said.

The second half of the concert was much delayed but thankfully uneventful.

"Fabulous! Bravo!" the audience shouted at the end.

"Talk about a concert with a difference!" a parent bawled. "How are you going to top this next term?"

"Loved that performance of *Sleigh Ride* from the orchestra!" another said.

"Wow! The winning carol was fantastic. It should be recorded for the BBC!"

The girls went wild, squealing and waving at their parents in the audience. I stood in a line with all the other music staff as we took a final bow.

"I think that's the last we'll see of Grace," Joe whispered.

"Poor woman," I said.

"Hank says she's going to be sent back to the States," Joe said. "She should get the psychiatric help she needs over there."

"That's good to hear," I said, "because I don't like seeing anyone that upset."

"I don't like thinking how upset you've been," he said, "when you got the wrong end of the stick again, this time about my sister."

"I can't believe you didn't realise," I said. "Look at it from my point of view..."

"I'd like to look at life not only from your point of view," Joe said, "but also with you. I missed you desperately all the time I was away...couldn't wait to get back to tell you how I felt..."

Suddenly a scream came from the back of the Hall.

"Three cheers for Miss Gold and the Music Department. Hip hip hooray, hip hip..."

Much later, when the audience had gone home and the girls had long ago made their way to their dormitories, Reverend Mother came over to me as I was busily tidying the Hall. "Well done, Flora dear. Another triumph!" Then she squeezed my shoulder and added, "And I'm so pleased for you, my dear."

"Yes," Sister Barbara said as she joined us and gave my shoulder another squeeze. "You make a lovely couple!"

As usual, I both appreciated the sentiments they were expressing, but also felt a little put out that nothing, absolutely nothing was secret at St. Cecilia's.

"You leave this to us," Reverend Mother said. "Sister Barbara and I will finish off here."

"Thank you," I said. "I'd better go and sort the Blue Parlour out, because I know the girls will have left the most terrible mess."

I met Susie and Hank as I left the Hall.

"It was brilliant, Flora," Hank said.

"Yes, and I loved being in the choir too," Susie added.

"Thank you," I said. "And Hank, do you think you might like to come and sing in the choir next term?"

"I think it's a distinct possibility," he said with a wink. "The way I feel at the moment, I don't care if I never go back to the States."

Wendy and Joe were already hard at work when I got to the Blue Parlour. There was so much stuff all over the floor – sheets of music, pencils, jumpers and the remnants of snacks. I had to tread carefully to avoid stepping in a lake of spilt squash.

Eventually, everything was shipshape. Wendy hugged me and squeezed my shoulder, giving me a meaningful look. What was it with everyone? My shoulder was getting quite sore.

Joe and I wandered out of the Blue Parlour to the Entrance Hall.

"I think I first fell in love with you when I saw you here," I said, "when you came for your interview."

"It took me a little longer," he said. "It was about an hour later – when we walked through the Hall after you'd shown me the Music Hut for the first time."

"I invited you to try the Steinway piano," I said.

"Yes! I played some jazzy chords in the bass and you improvised the catchiest tune over the top. Perfectly matched – perfectly in harmony. I knew then that I wanted to spend the rest of my life with you."

I reached out to him but he held up his hand.

"Not yet," he said. "There's something I have to ask you first. Hold your hand out – not that one –

the left. And close your eyes."

I did as I was told and heard a strange rustling and crinkling, then felt something tickly.

"According to legend," Joe said, "the ring finger has a vein that connects directly to the heart."

I looked at the fourth finger on my left hand; it wore a Hula Hoop and there were tiny grains of salt scattered over my fingers.

"I had to improvise," Joe said. "The girls left a half-empty packet of Hula Hoops on the floor of the Blue Parlour and I couldn't resist."

My heart hummed, whistled, then burst into a jaunty joyous song with full orchestral accompaniment, complete with military brass band, bells and cannon.

"Flora, my darling," Joe said. "We're so perfectly in tune with each other – will you be mine?"

About The Author

Jenny Worstall

Jenny is a writer and musician living in South London with her family. You will find her playing the piano, singing in a choir or gossiping with her friends (essential research for her writing).

She is a member of the Romantic Novelists' Association and the Society of Women Writers and Journalists.

Her writing reflects her love of music and a tendency not to take life too seriously.

If you have enjoyed this book or any other book by Jenny Worstall, why not leave a review on Amazon? It's easy to do and doesn't have to be long — who knows, you might help another reader discover Jenny's books!

Printed in Great Britain
by Amazon